He held her close to him.

"Go with it," Zac said.

"Did you change your mind?" Iris asked, staring into his blue eyes and hoping he had. Though part of her wanted him just for her own, this was easier. Not messy feelings, not falling for someone who thought she was basic. Just a simple exchange of favors.

"Yes," he said under his breath.

She wrapped her arms around his neck and planted the showiest kiss on his lips that she could. She knew it had to look good for the paparazzi and she put everything she had into it.

He dipped her low, his tongue sliding over hers and she forgot about the cameras and the game. Forgot everything but the fact that this man was holding her in his arms, and he made her feel alive.

* * *

Her One Night Proposal by Katherine Garbera is part of the One Night series.

Dear Reader,

Happy spring! I'm so excited for you to meet the Bisset family and their rivals, the Williamses. You met Mari's brothers in *One Night to Risk It All*, and now Zac Bisset is getting his own story.

Iris Collins is a woman who has it all. She's got a reality TV show that is a blend between the glam lifestyle of the Kardashians and the serene back-to-nature living of Martha Stewart. She has had a single-girl-in-the-city image for a while and is ready to transition to domestic diva. The only problem is that Iris can't find a man who fits her life. Getting dumped the Monday before she's maid of honor at a televised wedding throws her for a loop. But her sister plants the seed that maybe she should buy herself a date for the weekend.

It sounds too good to be true and a little bit ridiculous, so Iris isn't seriously considering it until she falls into Zac Bisset's arms and the paparazzi snap a photo of them.

But nothing is as simple as it seems, and both Zac and Iris let their guard down, feeling safe to be their authentic selves in the relationship since they both know it's ending. Isn't it funny how it's hard to be vulnerable in a relationship when the stakes are high? Neither Iris nor Zac are prepared for how much a four-day destination wedding in Nantucket will change their lives.

Happy reading!

Katherine Garbera

KATHERINE GARBERA

HER ONE NIGHT PROPOSAL

HARLEQUIN

DESIRE

HARLEQUIN®
DESIRE™

Recycling programs
for this product may
not exist in your area.

ISBN-13: 978-1-335-20906-1

Her One Night Proposal

Copyright © 2020 by Katherine Garbera

All rights reserved. No part of this book may be used or reproduced in
any manner whatsoever without written permission except in the case of
brief quotations embodied in critical articles and reviews.

This is a work of fiction. Names, characters, places and incidents
are either the product of the author's imagination or are used fictitiously.
Any resemblance to actual persons, living or dead, businesses,
companies, events or locales is entirely coincidental.

This edition published by arrangement with Harlequin Books S.A.

For questions and comments about the quality of this book,
please contact us at CustomerService@Harlequin.com.

Harlequin Enterprises ULC
22 Adelaide St. West, 40th Floor
Toronto, Ontario M5H 4E3, Canada
www.Harlequin.com

Printed in U.S.A.

Katherine Garbera is the *USA TODAY* bestselling author of more than ninety-five books. Her writing is known for its emotional punch and sizzling sensuality. She lives in the Midlands of the UK with the love of her life; her son, who recently graduated university; and a spoiled miniature dachshund. You can find her online at www.katherinegarbera.com and on Facebook, Twitter and Instagram.

Books by Katherine Garbera

Harlequin Desire

The Wild Caruthers Bachelors

Tycoon Cowboy's Baby Surprise
The Tycoon's Fiancée Deal
Craving His Best Friend's Ex

One Night

One Night with His Ex
One Night, Two Secrets
One Night to Risk It All
Her One Night Proposal

Visit her Author Profile page at Harlequin.com, or katherinegarbera.com, for more titles.

You can also find Katherine Garbera on Facebook, along with other Harlequin Desire authors, at Facebook.com/harlequindesireauthors.

For Rob, love of my life and my partner in crime.
I'm so glad to be sharing this journey with you.

Acknowledgments

I don't know that I would have finished this book on
time without my afternoon sprints with Renee Ryan,
Cindy Kirk and Nancy Robards Thompson.
Thank you for inspiring me to stay on track
and get my word count every day.

Also, a special thank-you to my editor,
Charles Griemsman, for his insight and judicious
editing that makes my books shine!

One

Lunch with her family was always one of the high-lights of Iris Collins's week. It was a Wednesday afternoon tradition that had started when she and her twin sister, Thea, were home from boarding school and had followed them into adulthood. They always dined at the club in her father's high-rise office building in the financial district of Boston. Hal Collins was the sole owner and proprietor of Collins Combined, a firm that focused on long-term investments in publicly traded companies.

Iris's phone pinged just as she entered the lobby of the building. She pulled it out of the pocket of her sheath dress and glanced down at the screen to see it was from her so-called boyfriend. She put the phone back in her pocket as her sister came over to hug her.

"I knew you'd be early. I figured I'd get here first so we could chat before Mom and Dad get here," Thea said. "We haven't talked since your trip with Graham. How'd it go?"

"Okay," Iris said.

"Just okay?"

Actually, less than okay if she were honest. During their Bermuda vacation, Graham had pushed her to be more adventurous in bed and that had ended badly. He'd gone down to the bar to drink all night while Iris had sat on the balcony alone listening to the waves. She was trying to keep things going with him until her college roommate's wedding in ten days' time. Graham was her plus one at all the events and she was a bridesmaid so it could get awkward if they broke up. She knew the bride, Adler Osborn, had planned for them to attend as a couple and the last thing that Iris wanted to do was add any extra stress for her friend.

Her phone pinged again, and her smart watch vibrated on her arm. She glanced down to see it was another message from Graham.

"Speak of the devil," she said, pulling her phone out to read the text while Thea looked over her shoulder.

Listen, things aren't working out between us, so I'm done with dating you. I hope you understand.

"Are you kidding me?" Thea said. "He's breaking up with you over a text."

Iris wished she could be surprised but was relieved instead. She quickly typed, Sure, I understand.

Great. Figured you'd get it.

"Get what?"

"Nothing," Iris said to her sister. The last thing she wanted to do was talk about sex in the lobby of their father's building. She was starting to wonder if she was the prude that Graham had labeled her... and did that matter to her?

Thea took her phone from her before she could stop her, typing in a quick message.

That's okay I want more from life than you can offer.

"Thea. Give me back my phone."

She saw the dancing dots that meant Graham was responding and her stomach felt tight. There was no way he was going to take that kind of insult without replying. That was just the kind of person he was.

That's okay I want someone who's not beige, boring and basic. Bye, bitch.

Thea reached for her phone, but Iris just held it away from her and texted back the thumbs-up emoji.

"Why did you do that?" Iris said to her sister. "He was my plus one. I'm going to have to deal with him not being there."

"Who do you have to deal with?" their mother

asked as she came up behind them and hugged them both. Always larger than life, Corinne Collins, known as Coco to her close friends and bridge group, was wearing Ralph Lauren.

"Graham. That guy I was dating."

"He just broke up with her over text," Thea added. "How rude."

"Very rude. But not everyone pays attention to etiquette these days."

"They don't," Iris said. "Where's Dad?"

"He's running late," Mom said. "I warned him not to be too late or I'm taking you two on a shopping spree."

They all laughed as it was a family joke between their parents from back in their early days when her father said time was money and her mom had said she agreed and liked to use her time to spend it.

As Iris followed her mom and her sister to the hostess stand at the entrance to the restaurant on the second floor, she was seething. How dare he say something so rude to her? Of course, she knew he thought she was boring...but basic? She was *so* not basic. She was Iris Collins, television lifestyle guru. Known for her trendsetting style and Instagram-worthy jet-setting.

She'd known he was douche bag when he'd suggested a three-way, but this was beyond.

Her mom saw a friend from her bridge club at the bar and went to chat with her, which meant that Thea and she were alone again.

"You need to bring someone so hot to the wedding. Show him who's basic. I can't believe he had the nerve to say that," Thea said.

"Agree. But who? I don't know anyone. I really don't have time to cultivate a relationship in only ten days."

"Let me think," Thea said.

"It can't be anyone I know," Iris added. Graham knew most of the people she worked with.

"True. You should hire someone. Just be straight-forward about it. Like a Julia Roberts movie. You can do that."

"No," Iris said.

"Why not?"

"Because it's embarrassing, that's why."

"It's not embarrassing. You could have a hot guy on your arm, and if you're footing the bill, he has to behave the way you want him to," Thea said. "I know some hot guys who might be interested."

"Like who? You work at home with two cats," Iris pointed out. Her sister ran a very successful blog about etiquette and deportment. There was a high demand for people who wanted to actually live the life in those swank Instagram photos they saw on-line, and Thea was in demand when it came to so-cial events.

"I have friends," Thea added.

"Thanks, Thea," she said. "But I'll sort this out. We don't need to waste any more time on Graham."

Their father arrived and they had a nice lunch. Iris had that feeling deep inside as she watched her parents holding hands under the table during coffee and dessert. That longing that she always felt. Was it too much to ask that she could find a partner? She wanted what they had but she seemed to attract men like Graham.

But for now, maybe Thea was right. She could find a hot guy to hire as her date for the wedding. It was only four days and three nights…

Zac Bisset hated being in Boston but there were times when real life intruded on his training schedule and he was forced to leave his yacht and deal with it. It didn't matter that it was a perfectly nice June day. He was wearing a suit and loafers instead of a pair of swim trunks and bare feet. Being born into a family that had wealth, privilege and way too many constrictions had never suited Zac well. He'd found his escape on the sea, sailing. It was a passion he'd pursued through his college years. Then he'd joined an America's Cup team from the UK and done that for the last few years, but he'd recently left the team to start his own bid.

Putting together an America's Cup team was expensive. He could easily ask for and receive the money from his family's company, Bisset Industries. But that money would come with too many strings. His father had been dying to get him to be more active on the board and the last thing Zac wanted was to answer to August Bisset. Or worse, his older brother Logan. He liked having the freedom to do his own thing.

But his options were limited. After the US-sponsored Oracle team won, Zac had craved creating his own team and putting together his own bid to win. He needed a big company to sponsor him or his own inheritance to make a successful run. Time was running out since they needed to already be training.

He left the meeting at the corporate offices of the large telecom company where he'd been discussing a sponsorship. When he got to the bar in the lobby and ordered a club soda, his phone pinged and then started buzzing as a slew of messages came in. The first was from his eldest brother, Darien, who was a politician and not in the family business; he wanted to meet up for drinks before their cousin's wedding festivities kicked off. Then there was a message from the group chat he had with his teammates who were waiting for an update. The last was from his mom, saying she was on Nantucket at Gran's place and urging him to come by early so they could have some mom-and-son time.

He rubbed the back of his neck, not interested in responding to any of them at the moment. Of course, his two favorite people in the family had reached out, which he appreciated. Logan and his dad wanted to boycott Adler's wedding because she was marrying into the Williams family. They were the chief competitors of Bisset Industries; their business had been started by a man his father hated. So there was that.

Zac had no beef with the groom, so he'd volunteered to go to all the events. He liked a wedding party. With booze, pretty girls and lots of dancing, it was his kind of shindig. It was a destination wedding, so everyone was being put up at a luxury resort on Nantucket, the flagship of Williams Inc.'s newest venture. The groom and his family were slowly encroaching on every line of business the Bissets were in. But Zac's youngest sibling and only sister, Mari, had been to a press party there a month ago and couldn't stop singing the resort's praises.

Which had done nothing to make Logan and his father happier about going. Family was trying at times and one of the reasons he preferred to stick to training for the America's Cup.

He texted his teammates first. They had a group chat nicknamed the Windjammers. The team was pretty small at the moment, just Zac, Yancy McNeil and Dev Kellman. The three of them were in New England searching for sponsors and working on a new design for their yacht. The competition was won as much with skill on the seas as it was with the aerodynamic design of the craft.

No-go on the money. Got one more meeting before we are going to have to brainstorm more options.

Yancy was the first to respond.

Damn. I have some feelers out. Heard from a friend that she has someone who is looking for a long-term investment. I'll text you the deets.

Dev quickly chimed in.

I don't have any leads but I do have some margaritas ready to go once you both get back to the Blind Faith.

Zac wrapped up the chat with, Thanks. I'll check out your lead, Yancy.

Yancy texted over the information as Zac signaled the waiter for a refill of his soda water. He glanced up, his breath catching in his throat as he saw the blond woman walking into the bar. She wore a formfitting dress with tiny sleeves that left her long arms bare. She was tan and fit, and she moved with confidence and purpose. Their eyes met and she stopped, her lips parting in a slight smile. Her eyes were blue like the seas around the southern island of New Zealand. Her mouth was…damn, all he could stare at now. Her upper lip was fuller than her bottom one and it seemed to him that she was very kissable. All he could think about was how her mouth would feel under his.

He stretched his legs under the table and looked away. Yeah, he'd been at sea for too long if his first thought when seeing a woman was kissing her. He needed to get himself under control before he was surrounded by family for a week.

He heard footsteps and looked up, expecting to see the waiter, but it was the woman. She smelled good up close like the summer blossoms in his mother's garden at the house in the Hamptons. She had a direct kind of gaze that he liked. He wasn't a timid man and he didn't always know how to deal with people who were. Up close he could see that her hair wasn't truly blond but darker shades of caramel were shot through it. It curled around her shoulders and he noticed how slim her neck was and the tiny necklace with a flower charm on it.

* * *

Iris was still thinking about her sister's outrageous advice as she went to the bar across town after lunch. She glanced around the room; it was midafternoon, and she was meeting her "glam squad" to go over her prep for the wedding in Nantucket. The fact that Adler's wedding was going to be televised and there would be lots of vloggers and online society gossip websites meant that she was going to have to be camera-ready at all times.

She'd built her own platform over the last five years, working her way up from an assistant to Leta Veerland to her having her own style television show. Leta had taken reality television by storm in the late 1990s and early 2000s, starting out by showcasing her sister Jaqs' bridal designs. She had set a standard that many young video channel content creators tried to emulate, with her style and advice on creating the perfect personal habitat. Iris had learned from Leta that she had to always look the part when she walked out her door, even if she was only going to the grocery store. If one of her viewers saw her acting or looking in a way that contradicted her brand image, then she'd lose her believability.

Thea texted to say she'd found a guy who would be her date for the entire weekend for a thousand dollars. She tucked her phone away, not at all interested in some guy her sister found for her.

She glanced around and didn't see her makeup artist, KT, and her stylist and personal assistant, Stephan, so she headed toward one of the tall tables in the back. She almost stumbled when she saw the hunky blond sitting in one of the large leather club chairs near the entrance. He had a clean-shaven, chiseled jaw. His hair was long and brushed the tops of his shoulders, but it was clean and lustrous and reminded her of a Viking…not the pillaging kind but the hot, yummy kind.

Make him an offer he can't refuse.

Thea's voice whispered through her head and she shook it to dispel her sister's ridiculous idea. It absolutely wasn't happening.

But now that Thea had planted the seed, Iris did sort of wonder if she could do it. She ran a multi-million-dollar business. She remembered something her mom had said when she had started to make real money as a social media influencer: *don't be afraid to pay people to do the things you need done.*

Technically there was nothing wrong with showing up at a destination wedding without a date. But the wedding was going to be televised. She was getting ready to launch a domestic goddess–themed range of products and a book. Everyone from her management team to her own staff were looking at the numbers that said she was stagnating while her competition made advances. People like Scarlet O'Malley, the heiress and social media influencer, who was now married and expecting her first child. Iris's peers—her competition—were moving on from single-girl-in-the-city to new-wife-and-mama and she was still stuck in…boring-and-basic land.

Ugh!

If she showed up with someone like the Viking

on her arm, it would be a boost to her social image, and it would give her a man to pose with. She could even frame it as a business deal...

He glanced up and caught her staring and she smiled at him. He winked and smiled back. She walked over to him. She wished she'd paid more attention to that movie her mom had made them watch on girls' night... *Indecent Proposal*. She needed to channel her best Robert Redford...or she could *Pretty Woman* him and be Richard Gere.

Confidence was key. She could be confident. Hadn't she convinced her parents to let her start her own YouTube channel when she was fourteen?

"Hello," she said. She'd charm the socks off him, she thought. Glancing down at his feet she saw he hadn't worn socks with his loafers. Fate was giving her a sign that she wouldn't mess this up.

"Hi. Want to join me?" he asked.

She glanced at her watch. She had about fifteen minutes until she'd have to call her team. And Thea's idea was there, nagging at her...though really, if she was going to do this, she had to stop thinking of it as Thea's idea.

"Sure, but only if you'll allow me to buy you a drink," she said.

"I'm never one to turn down a pretty lady," he said, standing and holding out a chair for her to join him.

"You aren't?" she asked.

"Not at all."

"Have you ever regretted that?" she asked. This man seemed daring, just like the Viking she'd compared him too, but she knew that she might be seeing what she wanted to see and not the real man.

"Never. Sometimes it has turned out differently than I anticipated but that's life, isn't it?"

"Your life maybe. I'm pretty much always following a plan," she said. She watched him, carefully trying to gauge his reaction. Was she seriously thinking about Thea's outrageous suggestion?

Yes. She was.

"I've never been one to follow a plan," he said.

"How does that work?"

"I go where the wind takes me," he said.

"The wind?"

"I'm a sailor and compete in yacht races," he said.

Hah, she thought. She'd known he was a Viking and instead of pillaging he was out there conquering the sea.

"Like the America's Cup?" she asked. She really didn't know that much about yachting.

"Exactly like that. I'm currently putting together a team and looking for investors for my bid in four years," he said.

He needed investors…

"Why are you asking?" he asked.

She took a deep breath. If she was going to do this then she wasn't going to find a better man than this guy. He looked good, he needed investors and she liked him. "I need a favor," she said.

"And only a stranger will do?" he asked.

She noticed he had a pile of papers on the table in front of him and as she glanced down, she recognized it as a prospectus—the kind of document someone looking for investors would use to showcase their product. She quickly looked away as he sat back down and straightened the papers, turning them facedown on the table.

"Sorry, didn't mean to read your stuff," she said.

"No problem. But you mentioned you need a favor. I'm already intrigued. Please sit down and then you can tell me all about it," he said.

She sat down, crossing her feet at her ankles and keeping her back straight. Her father had once said that posture was the first step to giving off the air of confidence. She swallowed and then took a deep breath. She had to be careful: sexual harassment went both ways and she didn't want to come across like she was propositioning him.

"I'm going to make you an offer that you can't refuse," she said. Wasn't that what Robert Redford had said? Was that right? Wasn't that the line?

"What are you, the Godfather?"

"No, I'm trying to say I need a man for the weekend, and if that prospectus is any indication you're looking for investors, you need some money, so… I'm making a mess of this."

"Is this an indecent proposal?"

Two

She blushed and blinked at him and then sat up even straighter and tipped her head to the side. "It's more of a business proposal that is personal in nature."

He'd been propositioned before but usually by women who wanted entrée into his jet-set world.

"I'm intrigued," he said. And he wasn't lying. This woman was beautiful. And though the fact that she was offering him money out of the blue was crazy, it was a nice fantasy to think of someone like her sponsoring his America's Cup bid, not a bloodless corporation or his controlling father.

"I'm going to a destination wedding and I need a date. It's four days, three nights, and I'm willing to invest in your project there in return for you accompanying me. It would be strictly for show. I'm not expecting you to do anything indecent."

"Too bad. I sort of liked the idea," he said. Funny, he was about to attend a wedding that was scheduled to run for the same amount of time. Was she attending Adler's wedding, too?

Her shoulders stiffened and she sat up even straighter if that were possible. He liked her, he realized. She was different from the sporty women he usually hung out with, and though she was polished and clearly moved in the same social circles he'd grown up in, she felt different.

"Well, that's not on the table," she said.

"Why are you hiring a guy?" he asked. Frankly she didn't seem like the type of woman who had to pay someone to be with her, and if she was, what was he missing?

"It's a long story," she said. "And I really don't want to get into all the details. Suffice it to say, I was dating someone, and he broke up with me and I don't want to go stag to this event. It's televised and I'm filming while I'm there so…"

"It's about image?" he asked, a bit disappointed because she'd seemed to be more real than that. But he'd been fooled before so he shouldn't be too surprised.

She shook her head. "Yes, but it's not what you think. It's my business. I'm a lifestyle guru… I have a show and line of products and my mentor's sister designed the wedding dress so I'm doing an entire behind-the-scenes thing. If it was just me and not all the other brand stuff, I wouldn't care."

"Who are you?" he asked. "I hope you don't mind me asking but I've been out of the country and spend most of my time on the water."

"I'm Iris Collins."

He had heard of her, mainly from his sister, Mari, who had mentioned her as someone she wanted to grow her brand to be like. Which Zac had freely admitted he had no clue about. "I'm Zac."

"Am I right in assuming you need investors for your America's Cup bid?"

"Yes, I'm trying to find investors to fund my run. I have some new people and ideas I want to try," Zac explained.

"I think I can help you with that," she said.

"Lifestyle guru-ing pays that well?"

"Very well," she said with a laugh. "Which is another reason why I really need to present the right image. It would mainly involve you dressing up and holding my hand. Maybe there'd be a kiss or two but I just need someone to be my partner at all the events."

He was 100 percent sure that his answer had to be no. He didn't need Carlton Mansford—his father's PR-spin doctor—to explain that hiring himself out as a date for the weekend wasn't going to play well if it ever got out. And he'd been a Bisset long enough to know that this kind of thing wouldn't stay a secret.

He had to come clean with her. Let her know he wasn't desperate for money.

"I…"

He trailed off. He wanted to let her know it was a no-go but didn't want to embarrass her. Under different circumstances he'd have asked her out to dinner, but this wasn't that time. He had a problematic wedding of his own to attend, and he needed to really focus on getting serious investors for his team, not a nice lady who had some money to pay him for a weekend together.

She gave him a wry smile. "Don't say anything else. I knew it was a long shot. My sister said I should be Richard Gere and find myself someone pretty to have on my arm."

"She's right. But I'm not that guy," he said.

She nodded. "Thank you for your time. And the drink is of course on me."

She got up and walked away with way more class and elegance than he knew he could ever muster. She held her head high and back straight as she went over to the bar area.

Then there was a commotion near the entrance, and he noticed a TV cameraman and several photographers entering as the seating hostess tried to stop them.

They made a beeline for Iris and Zac turned to watch them.

"Ms. Collins, rumor has it that you were dumped by Graham Winstead III?" one of the paparazzi shouted out. "Will this affect the launch of your new Domestic Goddess line? How can you claim to know anything about domestic bliss when you're—"

"Boys, please. Rumors are just that. Rumors. I'm not going to deign to answer them. As my father always says, keeping your ear close to the ground and listening is good business, repeating what you heard is asking for trouble."

Iris Collins smiled winningly at the cameras and then glanced at her watch. "I have to run. I'm meeting someone important."

She turned and started to walk past the paparazzi, but bumped into a table and lost her balance. Zac was on his feet before he had a chance to remind himself he'd already decided this was a bad idea.

But somehow watching her maintain her poise and dignity as she dealt with the gossip had made him forget that. He wanted to know more about this woman. He caught her and pulled her into his arms, looking down into her startled face.

"Angel face, I've got you," he said, making sure he only looked at her.

Angel face?

She clung to his big shoulders and automatically smiled but she was pretty sure she looked like Jared Leto's version of the Joker from *Suicide Squad*. Being ambushed in person wasn't something she'd ever get used to. She preferred to deal with this kind of gossip online when she could rant to her assistant, then just smile and type out a response. Even more embarrassing had been the fact that she knew that Zac had overheard it all.

She'd pretty much used up all of her stores of

bravado talking to the paparazzi and the last thing she wanted now was to make things worse. There was a knot in the pit of her stomach, and she was angry. And she couldn't help it; ever since she was a young girl, when she got mad, she cried. She blinked a number of times, refusing to let anyone see tears in her eyes.

Including Zac, but he seemed to get that she needed someone at her side. And here he was, holding her and calling her *angel face*. She had been doing photo-calls for her blog and TV show for the last five years so she was polished and professional or at least she hoped she was on the outside. Inside she wanted to hammer out the details. Did this mean he would come with her to the wedding?

"Thanks," she said, straightening back up. But he continued to hold her close to him.

"Go with it," he said.

"Did you change your mind?" she asked, staring into his blue eyes and hoping that he had. Though a part of her wanted him just for her own, this was easier. No messy feelings, no falling for someone who thought she was basic. Just a simple exchange of favors.

"Yes," he said under his breath.

She wrapped her arms around his neck and planted the biggest, juiciest, showiest kiss on his lips that she could. She knew it had to look good for the paparazzi and she put everything she had into it. She thought he was surprised at first, but then he dipped her low, his tongue sliding over hers, and she forgot about the cameras and the game. Forgot everything but the fact that this man was holding her in his arms, and he made her feel alive.

He straightened them both up and she still felt dazed. She had no problem ignoring the paparazzi, who were calling out questions to them as they walked out of the bar. He just sort of directed her and she followed. As soon as they were on the street, a large Bentley pulled up and a driver got out and opened the door.

"Sir."

"Malcolm," Zac said as he held the door open and she slid in the backseat.

As soon as the door closed behind them and they were on their way, she grabbed her phone and texted someone. Then she turned to him.

"Sorry, I was supposed to meet my hair and makeup people back there. I just texted them to cancel. Now what's going on? Who are you? Did you really agree to be my date for four days? I'm pretty sure you don't need the money…unless you're a professional gigolo—you're not, right?"

He rubbed his finger over his lips and just stared at her as if he couldn't stop thinking about their kiss. If she were 100 percent honest, she couldn't either, but she wanted to pretend nothing had happened. She was beige, right? She didn't kiss a stranger and feel instant passion like this. It was probably a fluke, she thought. Yeah, a total fluke.

"You asked me to help you out in exchange for investing in my project," he said. "I wasn't going to do it, but when I saw what you were up against, I couldn't resist."

"Are you doing this out of pity?" she asked. If so, she was turning into a total loser. She really should never have started this whole indecent-proposal thing.

"No, I'm doing it for money," he said, winking at her.

Damn, he was so handsome for a minute she just smiled back at him and then his words sunk in. "But do you need money? You're not a gigolo, are you?"

"I don't know anyone younger than my grandmother who uses that word."

"I don't like the term man-whore," she quipped. "Listen, just answer me. Do you take money from women to hang out with them?"

"Just you," he said.

He was being cute, and she couldn't blame him, but this situation had just gone from a jokey idea to reality and she was committed because those photos of the two of them were going to go viral. Having him by her side would seriously save her bacon, but at the same time it created a bunch of issues she and her team were going to have to deal with.

"Glad to know I'm special. Where are we going?" she asked as she realized the driver seemed to be making a big circle around downtown.

"Wherever you want to discuss this," he said. "Malcolm will keep driving until we give him a location, right?"

"Yes, sir. Ma'am, where should I take you?" the driver asked her, without taking his eyes from the road.

"Take us to Collins Commons," she said, naming her father's compound in the financial district. They could discuss the details in one of the conference rooms there. Her phone started blowing up with texts and she glanced at them. Her team wanting to know where she was and who that hottie was with her.

"What's at Collins Commons?" he asked.

"My father's office. We can discuss your project, my investment in it and what I will need from you this weekend," she said. "I think it's best to get that all in writing so that we don't have any confusion."

"This weekend?"

"Yes. The wedding is the Osborn-Williams one on Nantucket."

Zac stared at her for a long moment and seemed to be pondering something but he finally just took a deep breath and nodded more to himself than to her.

"Your dad does this kind of thing?" Zac asked.

"Investments and contracts, yes. Hiring a man for the weekend, no. I think I'm the first one in our family to do this."

Zac had to give her props for recovering quickly; he realized there was much more to Iris Collins than met the eye. She had handled the online-gossip-site stringers with more aplomb that he ever had. He had seen her mask slip only once and that was when he kissed her.

She was attending his cousin's wedding. He

should tell her who he was, but then she might not believe he really wanted outside investors. They were still essentially strangers and telling people he was a Bisset, had complicated his life in the past.

He knew the embrace was meant to be all show for the photographers, but he'd never been good at hiding the truth of who he was. He was ambitious and some would say militant when it came to what he wanted. But then he was a Bisset, and even though he hadn't gone into the family business, he'd brought the cutthroat Bisset drive with him to the world of competitive sailing.

But this was an entirely new situation and he was trying to be chill until he got the lay of the land. The conference room they were led to in the Collins Commons building was well appointed. Not unlike the massively impressive boardroom in the Bisset Industries headquarters in New York.

He knew that at some point he needed to clear up who he was, but not yet. He was enjoying this. She'd wrested control back from him, and though it was counter to his nature, there was something about her that fascinated him.

Maybe it was that for the first time since he'd left Team GB and came back to New England to start his own team, he wasn't facing a choice that he didn't want to make. He had always been the kind of man who forged his own path. He'd known from watching Larry Ellison's attempts to win the America's Cup with his Oracle backing that it wouldn't be easy. But he hadn't realized how hard it would be to convince investors to take a chance on him without Bisset Industries' money also backing him.

He had always been able to make things happen without his father's assistance. It had been a point of pride for him and now… Well, unless he missed his guess, Iris had the connections to the kind of investors he needed. All he had to do was be her date for a long weekend. Simple enough.

Except his family would be at this wedding and, though he kept his private life private, the kind of splashy relationship she wanted from him…might raise questions. He had to make some decisions quickly.

"Are you freaked out now?" she asked.

"Aren't you?" he countered.

"Yes. I am. Listen, you were so sweet to come to my rescue when I tripped, but I'm not sure you know what you've gotten into," she said.

He leaned back in the large leather chair and steepled his fingers across his chest in a move he'd seen his father make many times when facing an opponent in the boardroom. The fact that the opponent was usually his aunt or his mom had always made Zac smile, but right now he was glad to have that model to draw on.

"Tell me about it," he said.

She nodded and stood up, moving to the other side of the large boardroom table and pacing in front of the windows that looked down on Collins Commons. The summer sun was filtered through the tinted windows but still provided enough light for him to admire her slim silhouette.

"As I mentioned, I'm a lifestyle television personality. My career started with a blog, and I was a personal assistant to Leta Veerland. I'm not sure if you've heard of her," Iris said.

"I know her," he said.

Leta Veerland was on par with Martha Stewart. She'd built her career in the 1980s and '90s with her lifestyle books, monthly magazine and television show. Yeah, he'd heard of her. His mom had considered her the gold standard for entertaining and had emulated Leta Veerland at all her Hamptons summer parties and events.

"I figured. She's a household name. Anyway, she wanted to cut back on the show and I transitioned into it and brought a younger, fresh perspective— her words—to it. And people seemed to respond. So, I've been doing this for about seven years now. My market has been growing from single-girl-in-the-city to coupledom-and-settling-down—"

"But you're not in a couple?" he asked.

"Well, yes. I mean I was dating someone but that didn't work out. And I'd been teasing that I'd reveal my new guy at this wedding that I'm a bridesmaid in. I'm also promoting a new product launch for brides-to-be and new wives so…"

"It would look really bad if you showed up stag," he said. "Okay, that makes sense. So what exactly do you need from me if I do this?"

She turned around, and he noticed when she

talked business there was none of that sweetness to her. She had a very serious go-getter expression that reminded him a lot of his father and his brother Logan when they were going in to close a deal.

"If? The paparazzi just caught us embracing. I'm afraid it's you or no one else," she said. "We just need to work out a price."

He stood up and walked around the long conference table, taking his time. He had somehow gotten the upper hand and while he knew funding and financing an America's Cup bid was way too high a price to ask her to pay for four days as her "boyfriend," they were both in a position where there wasn't an out.

She didn't back up when he moved closer, not stopping until only an inch of space separated them. "I'm afraid what I need is very pricey."

Three

Coming home to Nantucket was always bittersweet for Juliette Bisset. She and her mother, Vivian, had continually had a difficult relationship when they were in the city but on Nantucket they'd always been strangely close. Maybe it was the beach-hair-don't-care attitude that seemed to infuse the island. Juliette had never really thought too much about it, had simply vowed she'd be less harsh if she had a daughter of her own, something she'd failed at.

Her younger sister, Musette, had loved it here as well when she was alive. She'd been gone almost twenty-five years now. Juliette still missed her even though during the last few years of Musette's life, it had been difficult to love her and not live with the constant fear that she was going to kill herself with her reckless lifestyle.

"I figured I'd find you out here."

Juliette turned around to see her niece, Adler, standing there. Musette's daughter. She was the reason the entire family was descending on the island.

Adler's was going to be a no-holds-barred, celebrity-studded, televised ceremony. And as if that wasn't enough to cause stress, she was also marrying into the family of Juliette's husband's business rival. It was completely insane and yet seemed perfectly normal considering she was Musette's daughter. A part of Juliette imagined her sister, who'd never like August Bisset, chuckling in glee at the fact that her daughter was marrying into his rival's family.

"I can't help thinking about your mom this week as we are all here for your wedding."

"Me too. I miss her," Adler said.

Juliette put her arm around Adler and hugged her close. "Me too. I feel like she's here with us."

"I hope so," Adler said. "That's one of the reasons why I picked Nantucket for the wedding. This is where we were always happiest when she was still alive."

"I'm hoping the gardenias bloom in time for my wedding bouquet," Adler said.

Juliette knew that Musette used to leave the blossoms in Adler's nursery when she was a little girl. "I'm sure they will."

Adler turned away to the other headstones in the private family cemetery. This land had been in the

Wallis family for six generations and most of their ancestors were buried here.

"Why is this gravestone blank?" Adler asked.

Juliette's stomach felt like lead and her throat tightened. That tiny gravestone held her deepest, darkest secret. "It's for a baby who was stillborn."

"Oh. That's sad. Was it Gran's?" Adler asked.

"No, it wasn't," Juliette said. "Let's get back up to the house before that storm blows in."

Adler slipped her arm through Juliette's as they walked back up the cobblestone path toward the house. Adler was talking about her wedding and the last-minute things she needed to do in the three days before all of her guests arrived. But Juliette's mind was elsewhere—back there with that tiny unmarked gravestone. There were times when she'd wished she'd never hidden that baby.

But there were other actions she'd taken…things that couldn't be undone, so her little stillborn baby boy would always be hidden there.

They went through the house's beachside entrance, switching their sandy shoes for slippers that the butler, Michael, thoughtfully left for them. As soon as they entered the hallway, Dylan, Vivian's corgi, ran toward them. Adler dropped down to her knees, petting Dylan and getting several sloppy kisses.

Juliette petted Dylan, as well.

"Nice walk, Juliette?" her mother asked as she entered the hallway. Vivian was in her seventies but looked younger. She wore a pair of slim-fitting white jeans and a chambray shirt that she had loosely tucked in on one side. While on Nantucket and in beach mode, she let her naturally curly blond hair actually stay curly instead of having it straightened by her lady's maid, Celeste, each morning. She held a martini glass in one hand, and as she came closer to Juliette, she reached over and gave her a loose hug.

Then her mom did the same with Adler but added an air kiss. Juliette had compared herself to others for so many years, and for a moment she started to let the old feelings of jealousy well up before she shoved them aside. She had a daughter of her own that she was finally getting close to. Something she'd never expected to happen at the ripe old age of sixty-one.

"Martini, girls?"

"Yes, ma'am," Adler said.

"Definitely," Juliette said. This weekend was going to be hard for her in more ways than one, but she was going to do her best to face it with charm and a smile firmly in place.

"When is August coming?" her mom asked when they were all seated in the sunroom.

"I'm not entirely sure. He and Logan have a meeting with a client this week and they will be coming together," Juliette said.

She and her husband were enjoying a new closeness since he'd stepped down and handed the reins of Bisset Industries over to their son, Logan.

"I hope Logan and Uncle August are nice," Adler said. "Zac promised he'd help me ride herd on his older brother, but you know how Logan can be."

"I do. He's so much like your uncle," Juliette said, trying not to let her mind linger too long on that thought.

"How pricey will it be for you to join me?" Iris asked Zac as they continued their negotiation. She was trying to stay focused on business but he smelled good and that kiss earlier... How she'd felt when he'd kissed her kept distracting her. Was it a fluke? That was the one thought that was going through her head.

His mouth continued to be a distraction. It was firm looking, but his lips had been so soft when he kissed her. Had she just imagined it? She wasn't sure that hiring a man to be her date at the wedding was a good idea. She'd barely kissed Zac and she was already losing her focus on the big prize. She had to hustle to stay ahead of the competition. And instead of worrying about that she was wondering about his kiss.

Focus, girl.

"I'm actually putting together my own team for the America's Cup."

She blinked. That wasn't what she'd been expecting to hear. She knew very little about the America's Cup except that the CEO of Oracle had won for the United States a few years ago and that it had taken him a lot of money and time. "Is that what you do for a living? Sailing? Or is this a new hobby?"

"Yes, it's my job. I have some other interests as well, but the bulk of my time is spent training and participating in yachting competitions around the world. I've been in Australia for the last few years and I had hoped to captain the team I'd been training with, but they went in a different direction and I'm not really that great at taking orders so I'm doing my own thing. I need investors to help sponsor us."

"Okay. I think I can help," she said. "Actually, my dad manages all of my investments and I think this might be something that he would be interested in. He's always trying to diversify but this is niche."

"It is," he said. "You want your dad to know you hired me?"

"No. What I'm now thinking is that you and I would be together the four days at the wedding and then, since this is going to be a big investment, could we possibly extend the arrangement for, say, three months to get through my new product launch? Then you could go off to do your yachting and we could drift apart but it won't look like it was just for the wedding," she said. Now that she knew what he wanted, it was easier to get her head where it needed to be. She turned away from him and moved to the sideboard where she knew pens and paper were kept.

She took two legal pads out and pens and then hit the intercom button on the phone and rang her father's assistant.

"Hello, Bran. It's Iris. Could we send some refreshments into the small conference room and I'll need some time on my dad's schedule in an hour or so," she said.

"Certainly, Iris. I'll get some fresh fruit and those

cookies you like sent up. Shall I also bring in cold beverages and some coffee?" he asked.

She looked over at Zac. "Do you want coffee?"

"That'd be great," he said.

"Yes, please. Coffee for two."

"Certainly, Iris," Bran said, hanging up.

She walked back to the table and pushed one of the pads of paper and a pen across to Zac, and then pulled out a chair for herself. He took the paper and pen, then came around and sat down next to her.

Dang, but he was impossible not to watch as he moved. He had a lithe, masculine grace. She was still staring when he sat down next to her.

"What are we doing?"

She shook her head. She had to get over this ridiculous attraction to him. He would be an employee like KT or Stephan. She had to treat him as such.

"I thought we could each write down the things we need. I know you already have a prospectus. Do you have a profit-and-loss sheet?"

"I do," he said.

"Good. How do you feel about the three months?"

"I'm not even sure what it is you want from me," he said.

"I need you to be my boyfriend in public. Take photos with me, of course. You'd have to give me permission to use them on all social platforms. There are four days of events at the wedding, so I'd want you there at all times by my side. Once the wedding is over, I'm thinking we'll need one or two dates a week, as well as some cute social media exchanges and maybe a couple of live videos so I can keep us relevant. My product launch is in six weeks and once it does, I'll be traveling and doing events. We won't be together so maybe we can do some exchanges on social media again and possibly, if it works for your schedule, you could fly out and meet me at one of my appearances. I will give you the full schedule so we can see if that works."

"Uh, I don't know about that. Being your boo for the weekend is one thing, but all that other stuff is a big commitment. I'll have to start hiring my team and get to work on having the yacht I've designed manufactured. My time is going to be pretty well spoken for. I can do the wedding but beyond that you are on your own."

"Forget it then. I need someone… Actually now that you were photographed with me, I need you, Mister… I don't know your last name," she said.

"It's Bisset. My dad is—"

"Mr. Bisset, I don't think we need to go into families right now. All I'm interested in is the details. I'm going to be giving you a large amount of money, you are going to have to work for it."

"You are investing in my racing team, Iris," he countered. "You will see a profit from it when I win. I'm doing this as a favor because I like you, angel face."

He leaned in closer and she felt the brush of his minty breath across her cheek. "I think you like me too or you wouldn't have suggested this in the first place."

* * *

Her skin was as soft as it looked and the more time he spent with Iris, the happier he was with his gut decision to help her out. He hadn't liked watching the paparazzi question her, but he knew that was in no small part due to the way that they had treated his own little sister, Mari. Mari had had an affair with a married man when she was younger, and the press had sniffed that story out and made her life a living hell for a while.

As much as he knew that everyone seemed to live for the latest tea, he didn't like it. His sister said that being in the spotlight meant taking the good with the bad, but he wasn't sure about that. And because he wasn't going to lie to himself, that kiss between him and Iris had been hot. Hell, hotter than he'd expected. He didn't want to just walk away. But hanging out with her at the wedding was one thing. Three months of fake dates and appearances would be hard to maintain.

He wasn't at the point in his life where he wanted to focus on anything but winning the America's Cup and that meant his next few years were taken. But she wasn't going to back down; he could easily read the determination in her eyes. And as she'd said, now that they'd been photographed together, it was either him or no one. And he didn't want to leave her in the lurch.

"I do like you," she said, at last, touching her finger to his lip and then drawing her hand back.

A tingle went through him at her touch.

"So then. Let's make this work," he said, shifting back because he couldn't allow this to be anything more than a business deal. He needed investors and unless she was lying—and Iris didn't strike him as a woman who would make things up—she could provide solid backing. This place belonged to her father; she had real money on the table. He would make the three-month arrangement work.

"Yes, let's," she said. "I'm going to make a list of every event I need you at for the next three months. You jot down your schedule, as well."

"Before we do that, shouldn't we make sure that your investors are on board?" he asked. "Or did you anticipate that it would just be yourself?"

"Um, yes, of course," she said. "Let me see what you have. I think an investment group would be better, but I'll ask my dad."

He handed her his prospectus and she started going over it, making notes off to one side of her notepad. He watched as she flipped through the prospectus and the profit-and-loss sheet. Finally she sat back. "Okay I think you've got a solid plan here. I'm not sure why you weren't able to secure investment on your own."

"Me neither," he said.

"I wanted to sort our part of the arrangement out first, but I think my dad is going to need some time to look into this. So let's get him in here and we can discuss that. Regardless of his opinion, I will be investing in your run."

"Why?"

"Because you are going to help me out," she said. "I like a man who honors his word, and from what I've read in this document, you are qualified and know what you're doing."

"I'm not looking for handouts."

"You're not getting it. I'm not a passive investor. I'll be looking for updates quarterly."

"You will?"

"Yup, but don't worry, you'll be hanging out with me a lot so I can keep up to date," she said, with a wink. She pushed her chair back and stood up, but he stopped her with his hand on her wrist.

That electric tingle went up his arm again and his touch drew her off balance. She started to fall and he caught her and steadied her as he stood up. "I don't want you to think you're the boss."

"Why not? I clearly am. I'm going to work up an employment contract for the next three months for our personal arrangement," she said. "And we will have the investment contract separately, okay? You were right. I don't want my dad to know about this. It would be better for everyone if it seemed like you were into me."

"I am," he said.

"Perfect, keep that up," she said. "I'll go get my dad."

"Not yet," he said.

"What? Why not?"

"Because you're giving me credit for being a much better actor than I really am," he said, putting his hand on her waist and waiting to see if she pulled away.

She didn't. Instead she tipped her head to the side, watching him with those wide brown eyes of hers. She nibbled on her lower lip as she waited, and he was struck again that she was two very different women. Strong and confident in business, a little shy and reserved personally. Which of course made a certain kind of sense when he thought about her asking to hire him for the weekend.

"I'm not sure this is a good idea," she said, putting her hand on his chest. But she didn't push him away.

"Why not?"

"We're *pretending* to be a couple," she said. "I don't want to blur the lines."

"We have to make it look real," he said. "If you push me away when I touch you, no one will buy the act."

She nibbled her lower lip again and he bit back a moan. She turned him on like no one he'd been with in a long time. But he was here for business. Which was part of the point he'd been trying to make to her. They had to appear to be lovers even though they were strangers.

He'd also been determined to make his own path and that had sometimes led him astray, but he had to be honest, this detour was the most interesting one he'd found himself on. Pretend boyfriend/lover to a lifestyle guru…who knew?

Four

"So, my daughter tells me you're putting together a group of investors for an America's Cup bid. I read Ellison's book. That's a risky venture," Hal Collins said. He wasn't a tall man, but he carried himself as if he were. There was a sharp intelligence in his gray-blue eyes and a hint of the warmth that Zac had glimpsed in Iris's. He also recognized where Iris got her confidence and backbone.

"Yes, sir," Zac said. "I've been on two teams since I graduated from college and have a lot of experience and knowledge."

He'd been in the boardroom with Iris for what felt like hours and now her father was here to determine if investing in Zac's America's Cup bid was viable.

"Good to hear," Hal said. "Why are you striking out on your own?"

"The honest answer?"

"Always," Hal said.

"I don't take orders well. I know how to win but when you're cashing a paycheck and not the man footing the bill, not everyone will listen. I'm tired of coming in second," Zac said. Hal reminded him a bit of his brother Logan, who would have asked the same sort of questions. Zac knew he had to prove himself to Hal and he was willing to do that.

"Understandable," Hal said. "I don't take orders well either. So how do you know Iris?"

He glanced over at her where she sat a couple of seats away from him and her father. Her eyes widened. They hadn't finished working out the details of the "favor" she wanted from him. "We're dating, sir. I think you should know that I started dating Iris before I knew she was your daughter, so in no way did that influence me."

Hal glanced at her. "I thought you were seeing someone else."

"I was, Dad, but that ended. Zac and I just met and hit it off," she said. "This isn't about my personal life. It's about a pretty solid investment. You are always urging me to diversify."

Hal looked like he didn't want to let the relationship questions go but he just nodded. "This is a risky investment, but from what I've read, I think you might be worth the risk. I need to do some more research, and I'm not sure when you need an answer?"

"The sooner the better. I have already started the design process and I have two team members, but I'll need to recruit more. To be successful in an America's Cup bid, the longer we have to train and prepare the better we will be."

"Fair enough," Hal said. "I should be able to have an answer for you tomorrow. Iris, will you still need the conference room?"

"If you don't, then yes. We're discussing a few details about our schedules," Iris said.

Hal seemed surprised that she'd choose a business setting for a personal matter and Zac knew they were going to end up answering more questions, so he just stood up. "Sorry, that's my fault, sir. I don't live in Boston and didn't want to suggest she go back to my hotel room to talk or to her house. As Iris mentioned, we've just started dating."

"I like that. The other guy was too pushy," Hal said, standing. Iris stood too and smiled at her father as he left the room, carrying all of Zac's financial information with him.

Zac realized he should have mentioned his father and his own fortune and made a quick decision. "I need a private word, Mr. Collins."

Iris seemed surprised and he wondered if she thought he was going to tell her dad about the offer she'd made him. But he just smiled as reassuringly as he could at Iris.

"I need to return some calls. I'll wait in the reception area, Dad."

Iris left the room as Hal sat back down.

"Are you August Bisset's son?" Hal asked.

"Yes."

"Why haven't you mentioned this to Iris?" Hal asked. "I'm not sure keeping this kind of secret is a good idea."

"It didn't come up, but I'm planning to tell her. As you know my family owns Bisset Industries and I have a large investment portfolio of my own. I'll be putting up some of my own money but I need outside investment."

"Why don't you just go to your brother and ask him to invest?" Hal said.

Zac wasn't surprised that Hal knew his brother, Logan, was the CEO of Bisset Industries. "I don't like the strings that come with that. I need to be free to do this on my own. I'm not saying I won't answer to investors, but when it comes to doing business with family...it's difficult."

"I've heard it can be," Hal said. "Thank you for telling me. I think you'd be safe telling Iris, but my wife has warned me not to interfere in either of my daughters' relationships."

"That's probably good advice. I will tell her but thought you might find it odd when you start doing your research and realize I didn't mention it," he said.

"Makes sense. I have a few investors who like long shots and can take the hit if we lose money. I was thinking of a five to six person investor group. We'd form it as an LLC and you would work for us. I know Iris wants to invest in you and you could put your money in through the LLC too," Hal said.

"That sounds like the right approach. And I've been working on a new cutting-edge design for the fin that I think we might be able to monetize after the race," he said.

"Good to know. I think we can at least get the ball rolling this week once I've done a bit more research," Hal said. This time when he stood, he held his hand out to Zac.

He shook the older man's hand, realizing that Iris had given him exactly what he'd been looking for. So he was going to have to give her what she'd asked for from him.

"I'll let Iris know we're done," Hal said. "I look forward to seeing more of you, Zac."

Hal left the room and Zac walked over to the window, staring out at the city. He felt just as hemmed in as he always did when he was on the land, but this trip had been full of the unexpected. And he definitely couldn't complain.

When Iris left the conference room, she rescheduled KT and Stephan for the next morning at seven o'clock, then went down the hall to the patio area. It was surrounded on three sides by glass walls. She looked out at the city, pretending that this was a normal day. But it wasn't. She had been on a roller coaster since she'd gotten that text from Graham.

Her phone pinged and she saw that it was a text from Adler. Her best friend, the bride-to-be. It was a photo of two martini glasses, captioned, Saving one for you.

She texted back that she needed a drink or two. Adler's response was immediate. You okay?

Yeah. I'll tell you all about it when I'm on the island. Won't be with Graham at the wedding... I'm too basic for him. Whatever, right?

He's a dick. Are you sure you're okay? Want to chat?

Can't at the moment.

She hesitated.

Believe it or not, I met a guy.

Good. Tell me more.

He's cute, really bright blue eyes, and he has a bit of stubble. You know, normally I'm opposed but it suits him. Also he kissed me, and it was way hotter than anything I've experienced before.

Sounds perfect. Are you bringing him to the wedding?

Yes. Is that okay?

It's fine. Can't wait to meet him. Text me after drinks and let me know how it went.

Will do.

Bran cleared his throat and she looked up.

"Your father said he's done speaking with Mr. Bisset and you can rejoin him," Bran said.

"Thank you. We shouldn't be much longer."

"Your father pays really good overtime so it's not a problem if you are," he joked.

She followed him back into the office area and then went down toward the conference room. On the walls of the hallway were photos from the different companies her father had invested in over the years. Some of them included her father as a younger man and in many of them her mom was by his side.

She felt a pang deep inside of her.

It wasn't that she needed a man to complete her or that she was less than without a guy at her elbow. It was that she wanted a partner. For some of the companies in the photos, she clearly remembered her father struggling to decide to invest in the firm and how her mom had been his sounding board. She knew the stakes because they were in it together.

Iris wanted that. She'd thought that Graham would be that kind of guy. He hadn't shied away from the social media aspect of her career, he liked that she made more money than he did and he'd been nice to have at events and functions. Despite being douchey at times, Graham was very good at a cocktail party. But he hadn't been right for her. She'd sort of sensed it from the first but then she'd put her misgivings aside, preferring to ignore the bad stuff and focus on the good.

But she'd deceived herself.

She wouldn't do that with Zac. He was really going to be just for show, and as much as her heart ached at the thought of that, her mind and her bruised spirit applauded it. How many hits could her soul take before she just turned into... Leta. As much as Iris loved her mentor, she'd had six failed marriages and was very cynical toward the opposite sex.

"Iris?"

She turned toward the conference room where Zac stood in the doorway. She smiled at him. "Just taking a stroll down memory lane. So much of my family is built into Collins Combined that it's hard not to sometimes feel nostalgic."

And envious, she admitted to herself. But then she straightened her shoulders. She wasn't big into feeling sorry for herself. She tucked her phone into the pocket of her dress and turned toward him. "Let's get down to business on this, shall we?"

"There's nothing more to discuss," he said. "I'll do what you've asked. I think it's fair. Your father is offering more than I'd expected from you when you suggested this exchange."

As much as she wanted to hear that news, she had to be sure he understood what she wanted. "Let's go in the conference room and make sure we both have the details the same."

He stopped her as he walked by him. With his hand on her upper arm, she looked up into his eyes and felt that heat running through her at his touch. She had to get this under control. Hadn't she just realized that by lying to herself she'd end up broken?

She had to stuff the attraction way down. She'd put her own personal needs and desires aside when she'd started on this path and it needed to stay that way.

She'd built her empire from showing people what they wanted to see and not by being herself. It was too late to change now. She didn't want to lose what she'd built and she had a feeling not keeping strict boundaries with Zac could spell trouble.

"I think we should only be touching when we're in public," she said. "Let's go inside and address this."

"Address what? You want me to be your—"

She put her hand over his mouth to stop him from saying anything else as she noticed her father's assistant coming out of his office.

Zac arched his eyebrows at her as she flushed and drew him into the conference room, closing the door firmly behind them and leaning back against it. She let her tingling hand drop from his mouth. She wasn't normally such a touchy person.

"Well, angel face, that was definitely touching."

Zac could see the conflict in her. There was something about her that was deeply sensual, yet she seemed to prefer to keep it hidden. It was there in her appearance. Her hair was pulled back low on her neck, her clothing was sensibly feminine and conservative, which only made her sensual mouth and her figure stand out more because there was a natural grace and femininity in every move she made.

"What did Dad say?" she asked.

"He's interested in putting together an LLC of five or six investors. You'd be one."

"Good. That works for me. Please, sit down, Mr. Bisset," she said.

"Is this the part where you explain that you're the boss?" he asked as he moved to one of the chairs. He wanted to tease her and see if he could find his way past the bow tied at her neck and maybe loosen up that hairstyle, but he needed to finalize their agreement more. He wanted to know the boundaries and parameters because he was ready to get back to his team and start the wheels in motion. He had no doubt that once Hal started researching both himself and his yacht-captaining career, he would get behind him. And even if he didn't, Zac had decided he'd fund the run himself. That was what Larry Ellison had done. But part of the reason Zac had hesitated to do that was ego. He wanted to know that others believed in him. So that his run was more about proving something to himself than to the world.

"It is," she said. "So here's the schedule for the wedding. I think those four days will be the most intense part of this. Then I just need a few dates after. As I suggested earlier, at first we'll do a couple a week, and then I have my book and product launches and you'll be doing your boat stuff, so we stay long distance—a long-distance couple."

He almost smiled at the way she cut herself off from saying lovers. It amused him that she was... well, the way she was. He should mention he knew

Adler but she was on a roll with her requirements so he decided to let it ride for now.

"Okay. For the wedding, I'll be your guy at all of the events. We can hold hands, kiss and do whatever else you think we should."

"Thank you for that. But maybe we should set a limit on the kissing—once a day," she said.

"No. We should both be acting the way we would in a real relationship if we're going to sell it. Your dad is way too savvy not to notice if we just kiss once a day. We need to be ourselves."

"Believe it or not, that is me," she said.

"Well it's not me," he countered. "This has to seem like we're both real people. I can't be someone you made up."

"And yet you are," she said testily.

"Having second thoughts?" he asked her.

"Yes. And third and fourth. And it all comes back to you."

He scooted around so that his chair faced hers and pulled her closer to him. "The only way this is going to work is if we are a team. We have to have each other's backs. If we're both playing our own game, it will show to everyone who we meet."

"A team?" she asked.

There was something more going on here than the conversation. He could see it in her eyes. "Yes. We have to be partners. We'll look at the events and make a plan that shows you and me in our best light."

"I… I really like that."

"Good. I know that we have an arrangement, but

I think we should try to be friends. That will be fun too. We can learn about each other and that will lend a realness to the relationship."

"It will," she said.

He saw her taking notes and wondered how many relationships she'd been in. Because the way she was acting, it didn't seem like she had a lot of experience. "Isn't that what you normally do when you start dating someone?"

She put her pen down and tucked a tendril of hair that had escaped her updo back behind her ear. "I don't know. Normally I date people I meet at an event. If they are an influencer, then we try to stage photos and go places where our viewers want to see us—"

"That's not what I'm talking about. The last guy you dated—didn't you get to know him?"

"Yes. But he wasn't who I thought he was," she said. "It's so crazy because on the surface we seemed like we were made for each other but behind closed doors... Well, I'm glad that we won't have to worry about any of that."

"What are you talking about?" Zac asked. He wasn't sure what had happened, but it didn't sound like it was pleasant.

"Nothing. I like this," she said, flipping to a blank sheet of paper on her notepad and writing with clean and neat strokes. When she was done, she turned the pad to him and handed it over. "Read this and let me know your thoughts."

He glanced down at the contract she'd written on

the legal pad. It stated a start date for their association, as she'd called it, and it stated an end date of three months from today. She listed out what she wanted from him and then left a blank for the dollar amount of her investment.

"Should we make sure we have chemistry before we try this?" he asked.

She nodded a few times. "Yes, you're right. We need to make sure we're believable as a couple."

He stood up. She did so as well and then held out her hand. He reached out to take it, then tugged her toward him and lowered his head for a kiss.

Five

She clung to his shoulders as every nerve ending in her body went on high alert. His lips were close but he wasn't kissing her but she was so close to those lips of his. And she needed to prove to herself that earlier had been a fluke. That she was the highly business-focused and driven woman with a low sex drive she'd always been.

So she shifted slightly, leaning up until her lips brushed his. That tingle started again in her lips and she saw his eyes widen slightly before he took control of the kiss. Oh, dear Lord, the man tasted so good. Better than anything she'd tasted before. She held on to his shoulders; they were strong and muscly, probably from all that time spent captaining a yacht.

She felt one of his hands on the small of her back

and the other at her waist. His fingers moved against her skin, caressing her as someone cleared his throat behind her.

Zac broke the kiss and straightened, turning them both so that the boardroom table was at their backs.

"Dad," Iris said. "Sorry about that. We were just wrapping up in here… I mean it's not what it—"

"Stop explaining, Iris. The last thing either of us wants is to discuss you kissing Zac," her father said.

Iris smiled because her father was right and it seemed like that kiss had lent authenticity to their story that they were dating. "Did you need one of us?"

"Actually, both of you," her father said.

"Both of us?"

"Yes. I spoke with your mom and mentioned I'd met Zac and she wants to meet him too. You know she hates when I know something she doesn't," her father said with a wink.

All the enjoyment Iris had had from the kiss and feeling like she'd fooled her dad went out the window and instead panic started to fill her stomach, making her queasy. Fooling Dad was one thing, but her mom? That was going to be very difficult.

"Oh, I wish we could, Dad, but I promised Adler we'd be on Nantucket in the morning, so Zac and I were going to have a quiet night in."

"That's perfect, sweetie," her father said. "Your mom invited you both to dinner. I think Thea will be there too."

Of course, she would be.

"Zac, will that be okay? I know you said you had a call you needed to make tonight," she said, hoping he'd pick up on her subtle hint and make an excuse so they could skip dinner.

"That's fine. My call can wait," he said, wrapping his arm around her waist and squeezing her close to his side. "I look forward to getting to know your family better."

"Great. That's settled then. I'll text your mom. Be at ours at six-thirty," Iris's father said.

He turned and walked out of the boardroom, closing the door behind him. Iris took a deep breath before turning to face Zac. Before she could say anything, he ripped the page off the legal pad. "We should have two of these so we each have one."

"What?" she asked, not even thinking about the contract. "Yes, of course. Why did you say yes to dinner?"

"If we can't fool your family at dinner, how are we going to make a lot of people buy us as a couple for four days?" he asked. He pulled the legal pad to him and started copying what she'd written word-for-word.

"It will be harder with my mom and Thea. Dad's easy because he only sees what he wants to. But Mom is shrewd, and you should know that Thea suggested I hire a guy for the weekend so she might try to trip you up."

"Thanks for the heads-up. See, this will be a good test run."

"Yeah, probably," Iris said. "I mean, yes."

She felt a little light-headed. Maybe it was that kiss he'd laid on her…or she'd laid on him.

"I'm sorry about that kiss," she said. "I know you meant for it to seem as if we had been kissing if my father came in. It won't happen again."

"I didn't mind at all. I was going to do more than just hold you. I wanted whoever entered to pay attention to us and not this," he said, gesturing to the legal pad. She saw he'd signed his name on both copies. "You sign now and we'll both have a copy."

She went over and signed the second one and then took it and folded it neatly into thirds so it would fit into her purse.

Then it occurred to her that there was no termination clause. "We didn't give ourselves an out."

"You said there was no other option than to see things through for the three months. I'm a man of my word," he said. "And I can tell that you are a smart lady. You won't back out."

She nodded. "Do you have a hotel in town?"

"Yeah, I've got a place," he said. "I have a car there too."

They exchanged phone numbers and she gave him her address. "Do you want to just meet at my parents'?"

"No. I'll pick you up. I think your dad is an old-fashioned kind of guy," Zac said.

"You're not wrong, but he gets that we live in a modern world," she said. "I'll take my car and meet you there."

"You know your family best so that sounds good," he said.

"Okay, so see you tonight," she said, then led the way out of the conference room. As they walked down the hall, she realized she'd said goodbye too soon and now she had to either figure out something to say to him or just walk awkwardly in silence next to him.

In the elevator, he hit the ground-floor button.

"Zac, thank you," she said.

"You're very welcome," he said.

"So how did you get the money for this?" Dev Kellman asked when Zac arrived back at his family's Boston home where he and his friends were staying while they tried to drum up financing. Yancy Mc-Neil was there as well, standing by the bar when he entered.

"Through Iris," Zac said. His friends had never heard him mention a girlfriend, so he figured he'd better start talking about her soon. From watching his sister—whose channel and media following were a lot smaller than Iris's—get dragged when she started dating Inigo, he knew that the attention he and Iris would receive was going to be a lot more intense.

"Who's Iris?" Dev asked as he pulled three long-neck bottles of beer from the fridge behind the mini bar, gave one to Yancy and held one up toward Zac. Zac nodded.

Who was Iris? His objective had been to get financing, and of course he was on the verge of securing it in the most bizarre way possible. Dev and he had been good friends for the last ten years, having met at boarding school. He knew that Iris only wanted the two of them to know about their arrangement and he was going to honor that, but he hadn't really thought through the logistics of being her for-hire man. He was going to have lie to his friends and family or just shut them down with a few terse words.

"The lady I'm dating," Zac said.

"Since when?" Dev asked. "We landed two days ago, and you broke up with Zara before we left Sydney so I don't think you had time to get—"

"Since none-of-your-business," he said. He wasn't about to start making up stories about the two of them and Dev and Yancy didn't really need the details.

"Okay, okay, don't get cranky. I was just asking. It's not like you to hook up with a woman this quickly."

"She's different," Zac said at last. "You know I'm not all touchy-feely and *let's talk about our emotions.*"

"Me neither. Just when you tie our business to a woman, I want to make sure it's a good decision."

Dev and he both. It was risky. Which was why he'd almost come clean with Hal. He wanted to make sure that the deal with Hal went through regardless of this thing with Iris.

"I'm being careful. The money isn't tied to me dating her."

"Fair enough, but you've got tons of money. Why not just use yours?" Yancy asked.

"I am. Her dad is an investment guy. He puts together groups of investors who go after different ventures. When I mentioned to Iris that I was in Boston trying to raise funds, she mentioned her father might be interested. She said that he was always looking for new things. I don't think this is quite what he had in mind when he said that, but he was game. He's doing some research and is putting together an investment team. I'll be one of the shareholders as will Iris," Zac said.

"Cool. How will it be structured?" Yancy asked.

"I'm not sure yet, but he mentioned an LLC. I want you and me as COOs so that we can be in charge of getting who we need in place. We should know in the next few days about the funding, but I think it's safe to start shopping for a design company that can manufacture our yacht," Zac said. "I mentioned that we are planning to sell our design after the next Cup run."

"The patent is in our names," Dev reminded him.

"They know that. They'd get a share of the profit but no intellectual property claim."

"Great. I'll get the ball rolling. I'm having dinner with some guys who might be interested in joining our team tonight and then we can meet tomorrow to talk more," Dev said.

"Let's meet next week on Nantucket. I've got to be there for Adler's wedding and Iris is a bridesmaid,"

Zac said. He really needed to tell her about his connection to Adler.

"Ah, so that's how you two met. Cool. Can't wait to meet her. Thanks for putting this together. I was really getting sick of having our ideas overlooked."

"You don't have to thank me. We're a team," Dev said. "I've got to go. Talk tomorrow."

He did the one-armed bro hug with Dev and Yancy that had become their habit, then his friends left and Zac was alone in the town house. He went up to his room and stood in front of his closet. It had been a while since he'd had to socialize with upper-class people so he wanted to look the part.

He had a closet of clothing that the staff kept clean at all times. He didn't know how casual or formal dinner at the Collinses' house would be. He opted for some dark trousers and a button-down shirt and paired it with some dress shoes.

He rubbed his hand over his beard. He kept it neatly trimmed but it was summer and hotter here than it had been in Australia, so should he shave? He'd leave it for tonight.

He showered and dressed, then headed to the address that Iris had given him. When he pulled into the large circle drive, there were two cars already parked there: a green VW Beetle and a sleek beige BMW. He parked behind them, got out of the car and walked up the drive. He had a bouquet of flowers he'd picked up on his way over and a bottle of wine he'd nicked from his parents' wine cellar.

Did he look like he was trying too hard to impress her?

He texted Iris that he was in front of the house, then rang the doorbell. He heard a dog barking, and then the door opened and Iris stood there. She wore a pair of white trousers and a halter-neck top that showed off her shoulders and collarbone. Her hair was down around her shoulders and her brown eyes were warm as she smiled at him.

He wasn't sure why it mattered but he really hoped he impressed her.

"So, when did you meet this guy?" Thea asked as they sat at the counter in her mother's kitchen. She'd arrived twenty minutes earlier and she was just full of questions tonight.

"A few days ago," Iris said, keeping it vague because she'd been so busy making sure they had a legal document that she'd forgotten the details of their cover story. "I didn't want to say anything earlier because I hadn't broken things off with Graham."

"It's kind of quick," her mom said. "But your father was impressed by him."

"He's that kind of guy," Iris said. There was something solid and formidable about Zac. He wasn't like Graham, who, though charming, had at times seemed like he was trying too hard.

"I'm not sure I believe that," Thea said. "Remember what we were talking about at lunch?"

"Thea," Iris said. "I told you that silly plan you had wasn't necessary. You just didn't trust me."

"Sorry, Iris," Thea said, her eyes growing wide. "I was trying to help you. You didn't mention him so I thought that jerk Graham was humiliating you."

"It's okay. I know you were just trying to protect me," Iris said.

"What are you two talking about?" her mom asked, mixing some Aperol spritz drinks for them.

"I suggested Iris hire a guy to act as her date for the wedding weekend. Graham kind of left her high and dry," Thea said. "But you knew that he wasn't right before that text, didn't you?"

"Yes. This weekend he was…well, not what I had hoped he'd be. So I'd already made plans to move on," Iris said.

Oh, God, this had to work, because if it ever came out that she'd hired Zac, she was going to lose a lot of followers. She'd never lied to her audience before. She might stage photos but it was always based in honesty.

Had she made a mistake?

The doorbell rang just as her phone buzzed. She glanced down to see it was a text from Zac. Thea looked at it too. Angel face, I'm here.

"I'll get it."

She left the kitchen and wiped her sweaty hands on her legs as she went down the hall. This would work. She had no choice but to make it work.

She took a deep breath and opened the door. Zac looked good. Damn good. He'd put on a dress shirt and had it neatly tucked into a pair of nice trousers that showed off his slim waist. He had put on dress shoes and socks and his hair was nicely styled. As he took off his aviator-style sunglasses, she realized the navy shirt made his blue eyes more brilliant.

"Hi."

"Hello. I need to talk to you about the wedding."

"Come in," she said. "We can do it later. Not in front of everyone."

Zac stepped into her parents' house as Riley, her mom's thirteen-year-old miniature dachshund, came running down the hall, dancing around Zac's feet and barking.

"Riley, shush," she said, bending to pet the dog.

Zac stooped down next to her and shifted the bouquet of flowers and the bottle of wine he'd brought to the same hand so he could pet the little dog.

"Hello, Riley," he said. Riley loved the attention and started licking Zac's hand. Then after a final pet, Riley trotted back down the hall to the large kitchen where Iris's mom and sister waited.

Iris and Zac stood up. "Thanks for coming tonight. Dad's still at work. Thea and Mom are anxious to meet you. I said we met two days ago."

"Good," he said. "I was in Australia before that."

"Oh, okay. I was on a weekend trip with my ex. They might ask. Maybe we should say we met at the bar today," she said.

"Sounds good."

"Yes."

"Perfect," he said. "You look nice."

"Thanks. So do you. That shirt makes your eyes seem even bluer than before," she said.

He smiled at the compliment. "Should I have shaved? My mom hates stubble, but I figured I didn't want to look like I was trying too hard. Your dad would notice."

"I like the beard," she said, lifting her hand to touch it. It was soft and abraded her fingers slightly.

"Iris, are you going to keep him in the foyer, or can we meet him?" Thea said from the end of the hall.

"We're coming." Iris turned to face her sister and led the way to where Thea was standing. "Zac Bisset, this is my sister, Thea."

"Nice to meet you," he said, holding out his hand.

"Nice to meet you too," Thea said. "Come meet Mom. She's made Aperol spritzes as an aperitif. Do you like those?"

"My brother Darien calls them Kool-Aid for grown-ups."

"He has a point. They are very easy to drink," Thea said.

"Mom, this is Zac. Zac, this is my mom, Corinne," Iris said.

"Nice to meet you, Corinne," Zac said. "These are for you."

He handed her mom the flowers and the wine, then gave her an air kiss on the cheek, which her mom returned. "Thank you, Zac."

"You're welcome. Thank you for inviting me to dinner," he said.

"I'm sure Hal told you that once he met the guy

Iris was seeing, I was curious and wanted to meet you too," her mom said.

"He did," Zac admitted.

"No use pretending that we aren't very curious about you," Corinne said.

"I'm an open book," Zac said. "I'm glad to have the chance to meet Iris's family too."

Oh, great. Zac was saying all the right things. And doing everything as if she'd handed him a script. She had to remember it was an act or it would be very easy to fall for him.

Six

Iris walked Zac out after drinks and dessert were over. He had enjoyed meeting her family and it was easy to tell that, despite her online presence and social media persona, Iris lived a very normal life behind-the-scenes.

Thea had done her best to try to trip him up but one thing in their favor was the fact that they'd simply just started dating. There weren't a lot of things a two-day old couple were expected to already know about each other.

"Thea was tough," he said as he leaned back against his car. The sky was clear, and though the stars weren't as visible here as they were in the middle of the ocean, it was still a beautiful night.

"She's a pain in the butt," Iris said. "But I think

this was really good practice. So I know I said we wouldn't need to be on Nantucket until Thursday but would you mind going over tomorrow? Adler wants to catch up and of course meet you before everything gets started. She's my bestie so she's curious."

"Not at all. Actually, about that—" he said. He probably should mention that Adler was his cousin at this point.

"Good," Iris interrupted. "I'm going to be bringing some staff with me so we could meet at the hotel in Nantucket or drive down together."

"Staff?" he asked. "Besides me?"

"Yes. I have a glam squad who makes sure I'm camera-ready. Also my production assistant will be there. Aside from my bridal duties, I'm going to be doing a few on-air interviews as part of the recorded show. You'll be free to do your own thing during that time."

"I didn't realize the wedding was going to be televised," Zac said. "I can't drive down with you. I have a meeting with my team tomorrow. I'll meet you at the hotel."

"Yes, it's part of a show that features destination weddings. Adler's wedding will kick it off. Because my reality TV show is pretty much *my life* and the events I attend, I'll be doing some live shoots that will be aired later. I want you in some of them but just to add flavor—that's the part we spoke about earlier."

"Of course," he said, but he really wished he'd paid better attention when they'd negotiated terms because this was sounding more like work than he'd imagined. "Do I need a glam squad?"

She laughed. "No. KT and Stephan will get you camera-ready if need them but I really want to just use shots of the two of us from the weekend in a montage. I don't want you to feel pressured especially since that isn't what you signed up for."

He was beginning to feel like he didn't know what he'd signed up for. Iris wasn't what he'd expected. She intrigued him and he wondered if he'd ever really figure her out. It had been easy to see her as the good daughter tonight but she had demonstrated a wicked sense of humor and her family did a lot of gentle teasing. It was very different from the formal meals he was used to when his father was present. Then everyone was polite and traded thinly veiled barbs. The dinner with the Collins family tonight reminded him more of the meals he had when it was just his mom and his siblings.

Hal Collins was a very different man than August Bisset. Where August was domineering and forceful, Hal was…somehow gentler but in no way less shrewd.

"Great. Will they be staying in the same suite as us?"

"No. Definitely not," she said. "I want us to be able to have some downtime when we can be ourselves."

"Angel face, I'm never not myself," he said.

"Is that true? Even when you told my dad that you were a fan of opera?" she asked.

"Well, I mean, I do like *The Magic Flute*," Zac said. "But you know how it is when you meet the parents. You don't insult things they love."

"Very true," she said. "It's a good thing you'll be in training, otherwise I think he might invite us to join them next time they go."

"I wouldn't mind at all. My mom loves opera as does my gran. On Sundays before brunch, they both would fill the house with music. Sometimes opera, sometimes jazz, and when we got old enough, rock."

"Sounds like a wonderful tradition," she said. "I would love to meet your family someday."

Uh, yeah. "About that."

"What?"

"I didn't want you to recognize my last name at first, but I'm actually Adler's cousin. My mom is Juliette Bisset, her aunt and godmother. You'll get to meet more of my family than you probably want to," he said.

"What?" she asked. "Why didn't you say anything tonight at dinner?"

"I was trying to let your family get to know me. Plus it's pretentious to introduce myself as August Bisset's son," he said.

"I get that, but you should have said something," she said. "Why do you need my dad to find investors then? Can't you fund the run yourself?"

She looked angry and hurt and he realized he should have handled this better. "I'm sorry, Iris. I never meant to hurt you."

"You didn't. This is a business arrangement. I just like to know all the facts. Does Dad know?"

"Yes, he recognized me and I didn't deny it."

"So why play games with me?" she asked.

He tipped his head back, looking up at the evening sky.

"I'm sorry. I didn't mean to hurt you. I could do it with the help of my father and my brother, Logan, the current CEO of the family business, but the truth is they both put too many strings on the money and I don't want to answer to them. I started captaining to find my own thing and if I asked them for money... it wouldn't be mine anymore."

She folded her arms under her breasts and narrowed her eyes as she studied him. "That makes a certain kind of sense. I felt the same way when I started my own brand. I had Leta's backing but I knew I wanted to establish myself before I went to Collins Combine for an investment. It was more fulfilling knowing I'd made it on my own."

"That's what I want," he said. "I'm very successful in my field on someone else's team but I want to be the captain of a winning America's Cup yacht and the only way I can do that is with your help."

"Is there anything else you are hiding?" she asked. "I don't what there to be any more surprises."

"Well, I'm not faking it when I kiss you."

"No. Don't do that. This will only work if we treat it like a temporary thing," she said. "I bought you for three months."

"Angel face, I don't work like that," he said. "I'm

not good at faking it and frankly, I'm better at it than you. You were way too tense at the beginning of the meal, waiting for me to—"

"I know," she said. "It's just my business and everything is on the line. I think I made a huge mistake but there's no going back."

Her honesty undid him. He was ready to push her until she admitted that they should sleep together, that the attraction between them was hotter than the sun on a summer's day. But he saw that she was confused by the attraction and this offer she'd made him, which was out of character for her.

He noticed the blinds shifting in the front room of the house and realized that they had been out here too long. "Someone's watching us. Want to go someplace and talk? I have a town house that's not far from here or we could go to a bar."

She sighed. "Okay. Is the town house an Airbnb?"

"No," he said. "It's one my family owns. We have property all over the world and the place in Boston is one my mom uses when she comes up here to visit my gran."

"There is so much I don't know about you," she said.

"That's fine. We've only been dating for two days," he reminded her. "You okay to follow me?"

"Yes. But text me the address in case we get separated."

The blinds at the front of the house were still askew so he leaned in, putting his hand on her waist. Then he kissed her gently on the cheek. "Just to allay any suspicions."

She sighed as her hands curled around his biceps. "I like kissing you too. That's why I don't want to do it too often."

"Let's talk about it at my place," he said. "Want to leave your car here? I can bring you back to get it later."

"No," she said.

He stepped back, putting his hands up. "Okay. Whatever you want."

"Let's go."

He waited for her to get into her beige BMW and then got into his car. He pulled around her in the large circle drive and she followed him the short distance to the town house. There was ample parking for two cars in the driveway and he led her into the house.

She paused in the entrance hall, looking at the picture of the Bissets on the left wall. It included his extended family and had been taken earlier this year when Mari had announced her engagement to Inigo Velasquez.

"I know your sister," Iris said. "Not well, but I do consider her a friend. The ripples from this arrangement we have just keep growing."

Iris shook her head and then walked past him into the house. "Which way to…wherever you want to talk?"

"Second door on the left, wall switch as soon as you enter. I'll be right behind you," he said.

She moved down the hall the way she had moved in the boardroom earlier. She was getting back into businesswoman mode and he was the first to admit he preferred her in relaxed mode. But she was in charge. She had concerns and worries that he knew nothing about and frankly, he didn't need to. They had a deal.

He'd almost forgotten it while they'd been at dinner. Her family had been so warm and welcoming he wanted to be the new boyfriend—for real. He wanted to somehow believe that if he—was what? Someone completely different? He couldn't fit into that domestic scene in any scenario that wasn't pretend. He spent most of his life on a yacht and he wasn't planning to stop anytime soon. His life was on boats.

She'd taken a seat on the leather sofa in the living room. As much as he wanted to sit next to her, he walked to the large chambray-colored armchair and sat down, putting his feet up on the hassock. "So…"

"Zac, I'm sorry that I've put you in this situation. And I'm not even sure why you agreed. I know you want investors and I sort of understand wanting to do this without your family's interference, but you didn't need to agree to my dating plan in order to make that happen," she said. "I think because we're going to be lying to everyone about our relationship, we need to be honest with each other. We need to be clear so that there are no misunderstandings. Does that sound agreeable to you?"

"Yes, it does," he said. "That's why I told you I'm hot for you."

Her eyes widened for the shortest second and then she nodded. "Me too. But that's a complication I'm not sure I'm ready to handle. To be fair, you should know that I'm not very good at sex."

He was shocked for a second. Then he shook his head. "I highly doubt you're not good. Both players share the responsibility for that."

"Uh, oh…okay," she said. Then she groaned. "Why did I even say that? Even though my reputation is for saying the right thing and hosting fab events, in my personal life… I'm not as together as all that."

"I like it. It's real. I bet your viewers would get it too," he said. "Have you thought about being yourself?"

She shook her head. "No one wants that. Sure, it would be amusing for a short while as a novelty but everyone wants you to stick to the image they have of you. Everyone."

She sounded very sure and he wondered who had been disappointed in the real Iris. But that wasn't a question he needed answered right now.

"What's next?"

Next? She had no idea. She needed to get focused and stop thinking about how strong his arms had felt under her fingers. Or how warm his breath had been on her cheek. Or how she'd wanted one more real kiss instead of that brush of his lips earlier.

"Let's get the wedding details sorted out," she said. "Then I think we can plan to meet on Nantucket tomorrow."

"Sounds good. What are the details?" he asked.

"You might already know them," she said. "Since

you're family-of-the-bride. Let me pull up the schedule Adler sent." Iris took out her phone and called up her calendar. "So next Thursday is the welcome lunch at her gran's—your gran's place, then the sailing competition around the harbor. I guess we should do well at that."

"We should since I'm captaining one of the yachts. Are you a good sailor?"

"I'm okayish. I really don't swim well, but I do like being on the water," she said. No use going into details of how she liked to get below deck with a few drinks to calm her nerves.

"Great. That will be fun," he said. "We can do some romantic things on the boat."

She just vaguely nodded. *Like what?* she wanted to know, but kept that question to herself. "Then there's the clambake in the evening. That's a really full day. I think we should just be clear about being a new couple, touchy but not over the top with the PDA. I mean, we want to be cute and romantic, not X-rated."

He crossed his arms over his chest and nodded his head a few times. "I can do that. Am I staying with you in your suite? Or do I need my own place?"

"I was thinking the suite," she said. "Unless we should just not be lovers…"

"We're not lovers," he reminded her.

"I know that. I mean, will it make me seem too prudish if I don't have you in my suite? It's got two rooms so you can stay with me, and we can let anyone who's inclined to dwell on it, think what they want."

He started laughing.

"What?"

"*Inclined to dwell on it*—are you kidding?"

"No. I mean, it was kind of fussy of me, wasn't it? If people are going to gossip, it's up to them what they think."

"I agree. So, what's on Friday?"

"The golf scramble. Adler is pairing up with her side of the wedding party so we'll be separated for that. Then we have the rehearsal and the rehearsal dinner. Saturday is the big event, so I'll be busy helping Adler get ready and then there's the sunset ceremony followed by dancing all night. Can you dance?"

"I can. Mom insisted I learn. She said women like dancing and a man who says he won't is a turnoff."

"I agree," Iris said. "All that's left is brunch on Sunday and then we head home. Where will you go?"

"I'll stay in Nantucket for a few days unless your father has the investors ready by Monday then I'll come back to Boston with you," he said. "We can see each other frequently until the money is ready and then I'll have to start putting things in motion."

"That's settled then," she said. "I'll forward you the schedule. Remember, I'll be doing some filming as I mentioned. I'll also probably do some photos for my social accounts so I'll need you for those, but I'll use the events we're at for a backdrop."

She put her phone back into her bag and looked around the living room. It was very traditional but with sort of homey touches. There was a large landscape painting of Boston Harbor on one wall and candid family photos on the table by the sofa. She couldn't help smiling at the one of a teenaged Zac standing at the helm of a yacht. "When did you start yachting?"

"When I was nine. It was either that or go with Logan and Darien to the summer internship at Bisset Industries. And…well, Dad and I butt heads a lot so Mom suggested I try sailing lessons, which I loved. She calls me her water baby… I'm a Pisces."

"I'm an Aries but everyone says I'm not typical of the sign," she said.

"Uh, whoever says that doesn't know you at all," he commented.

She stuck her tongue out at him. "I am a tad bossy."

"Yeah, that's one way of putting it," he said.

She liked him. There was a part of her, the one that still secretly longed for a partner, that wished this was real. But she knew she'd never have talked to him if it hadn't been for Thea's suggestion. And he'd never be here if she hadn't made her offer. It was the only kind of relationship she was good at. It was fun and easy because she knew what she was getting and that it would be ending.

Was that really all she was going to have with him?

It was disappointing but she was glad that she had the chance to know him. Because he was so different from the other men in her life. And he made her feel like she was different...well, not different so much as that she could be herself and that was okay.

She realized that she wasn't trying to impress him and she'd have never guessed that would be so freeing.

"I guess I'll be going. Thank you, Zac."

He stood up when she did, and she turned to walk toward the door but he stopped her.

"Angel face?"

"Yes?"

"One more thing," he said, pulling her into his arms and giving her the kiss she'd been craving all night.

Seven

She was so cute, and it had been pretty hard to resist kissing her. He'd been thinking about it all night as he'd watched her and her family interact. He'd grown up in a reasonably supportive household but what he'd seen at the Collins family dinner table was something he'd truly never experienced. There was real love in the family and though he and his siblings had a close bond, their father had always encouraged them to compete against each other. To prove themselves to him that they were the best of the Bisset children.

Darien had reacted by smoking a lot as a teenager and then just skipping the family business, to leave room for Logan who was a lion and had no trouble going in for the kill when he sensed a weakness. That had been the one reason why growing up Zac hadn't wanted to go to the office with his older brothers. As much as he'd wanted August Bisset's approval, he never wanted to have to cut down Darien or Logan to get it.

Kissing Iris made him rethink the entire agreement he'd made with her. He didn't want to be bound by a contract, and for the first time in his life, he felt like he was pretending to be something he wasn't. It didn't sit well with him. He lifted his head to stare down into her face. Her eyes were closed but as soon as he broke the kiss, they flew open.

She put her hand on her lips and then she stepped back. "Did I do something wrong? I'll tell you in all honesty I'm not that great at this. I mean, the posing and looking like I'm enjoying a romantic embrace I can handle but the real—"

He put his finger over her mouth to stem the words that she couldn't seem to control. "Angel face, you're so damned good that you're making me regret I only agreed to be your man temporarily."

She tipped her head to the side and smiled up at him. "Really?"

He nodded.

"You're way sweeter than I bet you let anyone see," she said.

"I'm not sweet," he said. "That's lust talking."

"Lust? Is it because you've been at sea for so long?" she asked.

It was odd to see the woman who had negotiated with him in the boardroom like she was preparing to win *Shark Tank* be so shy when it came to personal relationships. Then again, he knew that everyone dealt with intimacy in his or her own way. Normally he liked to make it a competition because he wasn't comfortable letting his guard down.

But he was quickly coming to realize that he couldn't make this a game. She wasn't the kind of player who would be able to handle this. And that changed everything for him. She wasn't what he'd expected; even dinner at her family's home hadn't been what he was used to. Maybe he should change his thinking and acknowledge that she wasn't going to fit in any mold he had for her.

She wasn't just the lifestyle guru with the perfect image and confidence to boot. She was real and that enchanted him as nothing else could. Maybe she was his siren, tempting him with something so outside of his normal world that he would unknowingly crash against the rocks to get to her.

But at this moment, he didn't care. His mind might be trying to send out a warning, but his hard-on wasn't having any part of it. He pulled her back into his arms. "This has nothing to do with our deal."

"Why not?"

"Because I want you regardless of that contract," he said. Also, he realized that as a Bisset he wasn't about to let someone else be in charge. He was a bit chagrined to realize he had more traits in common with his father than he wanted to admit.

"I don't... Will you still honor the bargain no matter what the outcome tonight?" she asked.

"Yes, of course," he said. "What kind of men have you—never mind—I really don't want to know. I'm not going to back out now."

"Okay," she said. "I want to say one more time—"

"Don't. Forget about whatever you've experienced in the past, Iris. We've never been together before and I feel like we should both be ready for whatever comes our way."

"Whatever," she said, and he saw a glimpse of the control freak he'd witnessed in the boardroom cross her expression. She closed her eyes and took a deep breath.

He realized thinking wasn't going to help her relax. She wanted him; he'd felt it in her kiss. But she was afraid to move forward.

He pulled her back inside his house and lifted her off her feet, carrying her down the hall to the living room. The room was in shadow when he put her on her feet in front of the French doors that led to the patio.

She tipped her head back as he kept his arms around her waist. "Okay, Google, play 'They Can't Take That Away' by Billie Holiday."

The home assistant acknowledged his request and the music started. He pulled Iris more fully into his arms, dancing with her in front of the doors that led to the backyard. He held her loosely because she wasn't the kind of woman who responded to grasping, greedy passion, at least at this point. There might come a time later in their relationship—he stopped himself from continuing with that thought. Their relationship had an expiration date. It would end. So there was no point in holding anything back.

He could be himself and he could enjoy all of her because there wasn't any expectation that they'd have more than this time together.

He lowered his head and their eyes met. Hers were dreamy, and for the first time since he'd met her, she seemed to be relaxed. Her guard was completely lowered, and he realized that she was probably thinking the same way as he was. That this moment was all they had. There were no consequences.

He put his thumb on her chin and tipped her head back a bit more so he could kiss her again. He swayed to the music and tried to ignore the white-hot passion that was making his blood flow heavier in his veins and hardening his erection. He tried not to focus on the fact that he could tell she wasn't wearing a padded bra because he felt her hard nipples pressed against his chest when she wrapped her arms around his neck and went up on her tiptoes to kiss him.

He tried to pretend that this was like every other first time he'd been with a woman, but his gut and his heart warned him that it wasn't. His mind wasn't engaged, had been shut down, and consequences and repercussions weren't a consideration. All he wanted was this night with Iris and to squeeze every bit of emotion from it and her that he could.

Iris had to get out of her own way, and once she was in Zac's arms as he danced her around the living room, she sort of did. Part of it was the magic of Billie Holiday—the song was so old-fashioned and such a standard that Iris felt no pressure to be overtly sexy or to bring it. But the other part was just about being with Zac. He sang under his breath as he danced them around the living room; his tone was a bit off-key, but it was endearing. Something less than perfect in the breathtakingly sexy man.

When he kissed her, she forgot everything. She stopped worrying about making sure she kept her stomach sucked in and didn't breathe too heavily. She forgot all the tips she'd read about how to turn a man on and just relaxed. Her skin was wonderfully sensitized and her heart felt like it was beating a bit too fast. When she wrapped her arms around his shoulders, going up on tiptoe to deepen the kiss, she felt the brush of his erection against her stomach. She rubbed against him and would have pulled back, but he made this groan deep in his throat and then reached down to cup her butt, lifting her higher against him so that she felt the tip of his hard-on against her feminine center.

She'd never felt anything like this with a man before. Sure, when she masturbated, she could get there but this was the first time that a kiss and a touch had completely overwhelmed her.

She suspected that Zac was slowly leading her along and she didn't care because it felt so good, so right and exactly like she'd always thought sex should be. It wasn't tongues shoved down her throat or hands that seemed to grasp and pinch her breasts just a little too hard. It was soft caresses and a kiss that she never wanted to end.

He shifted her in his arms as the music changed. It was that song "You Belong To Me." Her heartbeat increased, a warning briefly going off in her mind that he couldn't belong to her, not for long. But she shushed it. The last thing she wanted was to start thinking and lose the feelings that Zac was stirring to life inside of her. When he spun them around and lifted her into his arms again, the world tilted and shifted until she was lying on her back on the couch.

"Still happy to be here with me?" he asked.

She nodded. "Yes."

"Good. If I do anything that makes you uncomfortable, tell me," he said.

"Same."

He laughed in that big kind way of his and she couldn't help smiling back. "Honestly, there isn't anything you could ask me to do that I wouldn't."

"That sounds like a challenge," she said, but she knew she wouldn't dare let herself ask him for anything too risqué.

"I hope you take it up," he said. "But not tonight."

He undid the buttons on his shirt and shrugged out of it, putting it on the coffee table before he sat down on the couch, brushing against her hips. He reached for her sandals and removed first one and then the other.

She reached out to touch his chest. It was covered in a soft mat of blond hair that tickled her fingers when she ran them over his hot skin. His muscles underneath were hard and he bunched them as she touched him. She ran her finger around his nipple and watched it harden under her caress and felt her own nipples do the same.

She drew her finger down the center of his chest and felt the jagged, raised skin that indicated a scar. She leaned closer but in the low lighting there was no way to really see it. She wanted to know more about it, but not now. She let her finger drift lower, following the line of hair that tapered as it approached his belly button. He had the kind of washboard abs that she'd only ever seen in magazines or on TV.

He sat very still and let her explore to her heart's content, but she noticed his erection growing bigger as her touch neared his cock. Her fingers tingled with the need to touch him, but what if she did and he suddenly got impatient, bringing all of this exploring to an end?

She sighed and lowered her hand, tracing the fly of his dress slacks and feeling the hard ridge underneath. He canted his hips forward, thrusting his erection against her fingers, and she curved them around his shaft, stroking him through his pants.

She felt hot and creamy between her legs and she knew she wanted him. She also felt hollow and empty like she wanted him inside of her. It didn't matter that these magical feelings would disappear when that happened. She still craved the feel of him inside her. She shifted around on the couch, reached up under the skirt of her dress and removed her panties.

She tried to straddle him, but he stopped her.

"We aren't in a hurry," he said.

"I am," she admitted. "If we wait too long, this feeling might go away."

She moved awkwardly, because once she started talking, the self-consciousness she thought she'd banished was back. She tried to straddle his lap and lost her balance, falling backward. But he caught her in his arms and lifted her, his biceps flexing under her hands as he settled her on his lap.

"I've got you," he said.

She couldn't say for certain if there was a hint of promise in his words or if she was just imagining it, but she decided to just follow her gut and take it for what she wanted it to be. Take him for what she wanted him to be. The kind of lover she'd always dreamed of finding but never had.

She tunneled her fingers through his thick blond hair and lowered herself, taking his mouth the way she wished he'd take her.

Zac slid his hands up under Iris's skirt and cupped her naked butt as she deepened their kiss. He'd wanted to take this slow, wanted to do this at a pace that worked for her, but at this point he was past thinking about timing. He wanted her and each breath he took sharpened his desire.

He was so hot and hard that he felt like he was going to explode unless he got inside her. He drew her down against his hard-on, thrusting up against her, frustrated by the layers of fabric separating them. He reached between them, pushing her skirt up and out of his way, the backs of his fingers brushing against her warmth. She moaned and lifted her head. He touched her again, holding her with his palm, and she closed her eyes, her head falling back as she gyrated against his hand. When he touched her most intimate flesh, her hands on his shoulders tightened. She made little circular motions with her hips and he adjusted his touch until she was moving more rapidly against him. He shifted his hand lower and entered her with one finger and she threw her head back as he did and moaned much louder this time.

He let her ride his hand until she screamed his name and seemed to come against him. She collapsed against his chest and he held her for a moment before she reached between them and lowered his zipper. He stopped her with his hand on top of hers. If she touched his naked cock, he wasn't going to be able to think of anything but taking her and making her his.

"Are you on the pill?" he asked.

She hesitated and swallowed hard. "Yes. Of course."

"Okay, good. I've got condoms in the other room," he said. "Want me to use one?"

She chewed her lower lip between her teeth.

"I know it's not romantic but a minute of talking now is worth it," he reassured her.

"Yes, I would prefer you use one."

"Wrap your legs around my waist and your arms around my shoulders."

She did it and he stood up, putting his hands on her backside to keep her in place as he walked to the bedroom that was down the hall. He went to the bed and sat down so that she was still on his lap.

"They are in the nightstand."

She reached over and flicked on the lamp first and then opened the drawer. Every time she moved, she rubbed against him and it was all he could do not to twist his hips, find her opening with the tip of his erection and thrust up into her. He was reciting maritime law in his head to keep from doing it and when she finally held up the condom packet, he took it from her with more exuberance than finesse. She slipped back on his lap, closer to his knees, and he reached between them to put the condom on.

Once he had it on, she looked at his erection and then back up at him. He wasn't sure what he read in her expression, but he almost felt like she was unsure again.

Damn.

"Do you still want to do this?" he asked. His voice sounded almost guttural since he was so turned on. Stopping was going to be hard but he'd do it because he never wanted to see fear or disgust on Iris's face.

"Yes," she said, putting her hands on either side of his face and lowering her mouth to kiss him again. She shifted and the skirt of her dress brushed over him. He bunched it in his fist and lifted it all the way up and out of the way. She shifted around, then reached between them to position him between her legs. She opened her eyes and their gazes met as she drove herself down on him.

Damn.

She fit him so tightly, like the best kind of glove,

and he wanted more. He had intended to let her set the pace, but he couldn't. He fell back on the bed and rolled over so she was under him. She held on to his shoulders as he brought his lips down hard on hers and thrust his tongue into her mouth. She sucked it hard as he drove up into her, taking her at a pace that was faster and harder than he'd intended. His conscience made him slow down and he started to pull back but she tightened her grip on him and whispered in his ear, "Don't stop."

He didn't stop. He just kept thrusting inside her until he heard those cries he'd heard when she'd orgasmed earlier as she came again he felt her body tightening around his. He drove himself faster and faster into her until he came in one long rush, emptying himself inside of her. He kept thrusting until he was sated and rolled to his side, pulling her into his arms and stroking her back while his heartbeat slowed.

She put her hand on his chest and then rested her head on top of it. She sighed and he lifted his head to look down at her.

"What?"

"Thanks for that. I have to be honest and tell you I wasn't expecting…"

He waited to see what else she'd say. It was clear to him that she hadn't enjoyed sex in the past, but he doubted she wanted to discuss that with him.

"What?" he asked again.

"You."

She rolled to her side and sat up after saying that.

Then she got off the bed and went to the bathroom. He watched her go, very aware that she wasn't the only one who'd been caught off guard tonight.

He hadn't been expecting her either.

Eight

Arriving on Nantucket one week later made Iris feel like she was in total vacay mode. It didn't matter that her glam squad had gotten her ready early this morning at her place in Boston to make sure she was casual yet sophisticated or that she had fifteen minutes before she had to meet the photographer on the beach to do a photo shoot for the summer social media shares. As she stood on the balcony of her hotel suite, listening to the crashing of the waves on the beach and smelling the salty air, she felt like she could breathe.

Sleeping with Zac hadn't been her best idea, she knew that, but damn, for the first time in her life she'd felt more than just the urge to get it over with when she'd been having sex. Zac had made her real-

ize that something she'd thought she could live without—an active sex life—wasn't true. She'd had no
idea that the men she'd been with hadn't been good
lovers. To be fair, it could have been that she wasn't
a right fit for those men.

Did that mean she was a right fit for Zac?

Or was it simply because she'd hired him for the
weekend that she had relaxed? She wished she could
talk to Adler and tell her the truth about what was
going on. But she didn't want anyone to know she'd
hired herself a man for the weekend.

Her phone pinged and she glanced at it. It was a
text from Adler.

Hey, girl! Are you on the island?

Just got in. I have a photo shoot in about ten minutes but want to catch up after?

Yes. Where's the photo shoot? I'll come by and
watch.

Private beach two houses down from your gran's
place.

See ya there. Is the new guy with you?

He had a few meetings this morning. He'll be here
this afternoon.

Perfect. Want to have dinner with Nick and me tonight?

Let me double-check with him.

Iris took a deep breath. This was what she needed to happen. She wanted people in her life to accept Zac as her real boyfriend. And he'd agreed to do whatever she asked for the weekend. She texted to ask if he'd be available around six for dinner. He responded with the thumbs-up. She let Adler know they'd both be there.

Should she mention to Adler that the man she was dating was her cousin? She wanted to tell her in person rather than over the phone. That kind of conversation was going to bring up all kinds of questions about Zac. She tossed her phone on the bed and fell back on the covers, staring at the pristine white ceiling as if she looked hard enough, she'd find some cosmic answer to the question.

There was a knock on her door and she hopped up to go and answer it. It was KT from her glam squad. KT always looked so boho and chic, with her long legs and straight brown hair that she'd styled in a side braid today. She wore a pair of tiny denim shorts with a flouncy top. It was a look that Iris envied but she had never been able to pull off. She was too intense for that kind of outfit. By contrast, she wore a broderie white sundress with wooden buttons and a pair of Hermès sandals.

"Parking is a bear near the beach," KT said. "We should leave now. Stephan is already there and the photographer is setting up."

"I hope the weather holds out," Iris said, grabbing

her phone and purse and leading the way out of the room. "There were storms yesterday."

"It's gorg out there today. As soon as your photo shoot is over, I'm going for a run on the beach."

"Sounds like a plan. I shouldn't need you until tomorrow for the clambake. I have the outfit you styled for me and know how to do my paddle-boarding makeup… I really hope I don't fall off the board. Did you see that can happen?"

Her assistant put her arm around Iris's shoulders. Everyone in her inner circle knew she struggled with a fear of water. She was slowly getting over it but there were times when it became overwhelming.

"You'll be fine. My sister says the key to paddle-boarding is a strong core," KT said.

"A strong core? I'm wearing Spanx 24/7. My core isn't soft at all."

"You'll do fine," KT said. "I've never known you to fail when you put your mind to something. Just remember that your followers are watching and want you to succeed. You're living that hashtag best life."

"I am, aren't I? Also the camera crew will be shooting the paddleboarding so I have that as an added incentive to stay on."

"Perfect. Plus, you'll want to impress your new man," KT said. "You're usually all about keeping up the perfect image so I know you'll do fine."

The perfect image. Was that what she was all about? "Do you think that comes off as me trying too hard?"

"Girl, it's your brand. I think it suits you." KT

followed her out of the resort to her car and they both got in.

Iris wanted to be chill about everything that KT had said but it was stirring up the thought that maybe she had been trying too hard for so long that even she didn't know how to relax and just be herself. That brought her back to sex with Zac... Had it been Zac and his fabulously fit body and sensual moves that had been the difference or the fact that she hadn't been trying to be who she thought he wanted her to be?

The answer wasn't going to just show up. Plus, did it matter? He was only with her until Sunday and then for a few more dates and photos before he was out of her life for good. She'd be back to her usual self. Which was exactly what she wanted. Truly.

Now if only she could convince herself of that.

Zac left Boston late, got stuck in traffic, and when he finally arrived on Nantucket, he was ready for a beer or two. He and Dev had spent most of the day on the phone or on Skype calls talking to people that they wanted on their team. Most were excited at the prospect of a new team, but a few were skeptical that they would be able to pull off a winning run with only two years to get the team going.

Zac wasn't interested in naysayers or nonbelievers, so even when Dev had argued to keep a few of the skeptics in the potential pool, Zac had cut them. If he'd learned one lesson from his father, it was to surround himself only with people who had the same goals. His dad had often said if a person was wishy-washy before you shook hands, they weren't going to become more committed after the deal was done.

He rubbed the back of his neck as he followed the map to the hotel where he'd be staying with Iris for the next few days, which he realized was going to be awkward for everyone if he didn't let his mom know. He thought about texting but she would only call him back so he used the hands-free voice command to dial her number.

"Hello, honey. Where are you?" his mom asked when she answered the phone.

"Just got off the ferry," he answered her.

"That's great. Shall we set a place for you at dinner?"

"Not tonight," he said. "I'm not going to stay at Gran's either."

"Why not?" she asked.

All of the sweet chattiness was now gone from her voice. She'd sent all of them an itinerary for Adler's wedding and she'd been very clear that she expected them to show up to all of the events on it.

"I met a woman in Boston, Mom. Turns out she's a friend of Adler's and I'm going to be staying with her."

"Wow, that's quick work," his mom said. "Who is she?"

"Iris Collins."

"Oh, I thought she was dating someone else. She's really nice. How did you meet her?" she asked, chatty again now that she knew he was with Iris.

Zac had never realized what a difference dating a woman who was in his social circle would make.

He'd pretty much always picked someone who was in the world of competitive yachting because those were the women he knew the best, so this was a new experience. He wondered if this was how Mari felt when she'd gotten engaged to Inigo Velasquez. The Formula One driver was definitely on Juliette Bisset's approved list.

"We met in a bar," he said.

"Oh," his mom said.

"*Oh?* Don't be judgy, Mom. You and Dad met at a weekend house party," he said. "I'm sure there were drinks served there."

"Did I sound judgy? I didn't mean to be. I was just hoping that you would have a meet-cute story."

"We don't live in a rom-com," he said.

"I know. I just always hope that all of my kids will have a big romance and Iris is definitely a step up—"

"Mom, I'm a second away from driving through a make-believe tunnel and losing my signal with you," he warned her.

"Point taken. Bring her with you to lunch tomorrow. Your father wants us to host the Williamses. Did you see my text?"

"I did and I will. I love you, Mom. I'll talk to you tomorrow," he said.

"Bye, sweetie, love you too."

She disconnected the call and he continued to make his way toward the hotel. His mom was not going to be very happy with him when he and Iris broke up. But that was a problem for Future Zac to deal with. Right now his mom was pleased that he'd landed someone like Iris. He wondered if he could have done it if she hadn't been desperate for a date. He liked to think so, but he wasn't sure.

He didn't know what kind of guy she usually went for but he was pretty sure she didn't often go for athletes or, as his dad like to refer to him, sea bums.

That night together last week, though... If he'd really been dating her that would have changed things for real between them. Instead he had no clue what it had done. He wasn't thinking of when he'd be able to walk away from her. In fact he'd been remembering how she'd felt in his arms all day at odd moments. Dev had accused him of losing focus, but Zac knew that his focus was fine.

It was just on Iris and not on the race or his yacht or the team he was building. Maybe there had been more of a reason to stay away from women in his own social set before this. After all, a sailor would know the score. A fellow sailor would know that he was only interested in having fun until the wind changed, and he was back on the ocean pitting himself against all the other crafts out there. Trying to be number one and conquer the sea.

He followed the signs to the hotel, pulling into line for the valet. As he did, he remembered that little sound that Iris had made when he'd entered her and the surprise on her face when she'd come long and hard. He wanted to see that look on her face again. He couldn't wait to hold her again.

Damn.

He was screwed.

It was a good thing that they had a signed contract. Otherwise he'd be tempted into thinking that Iris was the kind of woman who could make him stay ashore.

He stepped outside into the humid summer afternoon, blaming his agitation on the heat instead of the woman who'd paid him to be her companion.

Adler Osborn stood on the widow's walk and looked out at the storms brewing on the ocean. Only three more days until she'd be Mrs. Nicholas Williams and she couldn't wait. She'd had a text from her fiancé that he was en route and would meet her at the Crab Shack in town in twenty minutes. She couldn't wait to see Nick.

Growing up, her life had been unconventional to say the least. She'd never known her mother, who'd died when she was twenty-five and her father was a famous rock star who truly lived the sex, drugs and rock 'n' roll lifestyle, but also had oddly been a devoted parent. He wanted her with him on the road but her mother's family had wanted her attending the right schools and getting the proper upbringing.

Her Aunt Juliette and Gran had been fierce negotiators with her father, and they'd worked out a deal where she'd split time between two vastly different worlds. Though she loved both halves of her family very much, she'd always longed to be part of one world. It was hard to go from boarding school and socializing with a lot of rules to life on the road and no rules.

Until college, when she'd met Iris Collins and the two had become best friends, Adler had felt torn in half by her two lives. But Iris had helped her sort herself out. One of the things that Adler had realized was that she wanted all those things she'd never had growing up. A proper home—not a boarding school or tour bus. A home that she came back to every single night. A family that was her own. She wanted a husband, kids and the whole suburban life. But she needed someone who could understand her. Really got her. Not a guy who wanted entrée into her father's debauched world. Or who wanted to attend the jet-set parties her Aunt Juliette threw.

Nick Williams had been perfect. A borderline workaholic who was rich as Jay-Z and didn't give a crap about what anyone thought. He was fun, had the prettiest blue eyes she'd ever seen and the sexiest ass. When she'd first met him, she'd been dazzled. And it was only when things got rough for her, with her father's heart attack, and she found Nick standing by her side, putting work on the back burner to be there for her, that she realized that she'd found the man she wanted for the rest of her life.

She was no longer the illegitimate daughter of a debauched rock star and the runaway heiress who died of a drug overdose, but a respectable member of society. Someone who stayed out of the headlines and lived a normal life.

Gran had said that normal was overrated but then again Gran had been normal her entire life. Adler, not so much. And Iris was another one who lived and breathed for small-town suburbia…the dream, as far as Adler was concerned.

She texted Nick that Iris and her new man were meeting them. He rang back instead of texting.

"Hey, sexy!"

"Hey, gorgeous. Who's the new guy? I thought she was dating Douchey the Third," Nick said.

"I don't have the deets but he arrived about thirty minutes ago and I invited them to join us for dinner. I want to meet him and thought it would be weird if I just showed up in her hotel suite alone."

Nick laughed. "You might seem like a one-woman interrogation squad."

"I know. So, I thought if we met them together, then you could help make sure he's nothing like Douchey."

"Good plan. Am I picking you up?"

"Nah. Uncle Auggie has just arrived and I think I'll spare us that," she said. Her uncle didn't like her fiancé, which didn't bother Adler because she'd never been a big fan of her uncle. The fact that he'd cheated on her Aunt Juliette hadn't made him Gran's favorite either.

"Thanks for that. You can never doubt that I really love you, gorgeous, because there is no way I'd put up with August Bisset otherwise."

"I know it," she said, feeling her heart fill with joy. "See ya soon."

"See ya," he said, disconnecting the call.

Adler checked her makeup and then grabbed her clutch and headed downstairs. Michael was carrying his silver tray with two martinis and a bourbon neat to the sitting room.

"Will you be joining the others?"

"Nope. Heading out for the evening. I'll probably stay over at Nick's tonight," she said. Since Nick wasn't comfortable staying at her gran's place, he'd purchased a cottage for them that was two streets over. That way she could see the family she loved, and he didn't have to.

"Heading out, dear?" Gran called as Adler walked past the sitting room.

Her Uncle August was sitting in the large leather armchair and had his back to her. His hair was mostly gray now but at one time it had been black. He turned and smiled at her.

"Hello, Adler. Juliette was just telling me that you're all set for the wedding," he said.

"I'm getting there. Still a few last-minute things to take care of," she said, coming over to give him a hug. The thing about Uncle Auggie was that he wasn't a jerk. He was charming and fun. As her Aunt Juliette said, he was hard to stay mad at.

"If there's anything I can do, let me know," he said, then took a deep breath. "I know that there's some tension because of the business dealings Logan and I have had with your fiancé and I want to put that behind us. We'd like to have Nick and his family to dinner tomorrow night. Just so we can all get to know each other. Put everyone's mind's at ease."

Adler was surprised by the offer. "Let me speak to Nick tonight and let him know. That should work with our schedule since most people aren't arriving until Thursday."

"Great," he said, sitting back down. "I'll get Carter to make all the arrangements."

"I'll handle this, Auggie," Aunt Juliette said. "Have fun tonight, Adler. See you tomorrow?"

"Yes," she said, kissing her gran and aunt on the cheek before she turned and left the house.

Her uncle's gesture was surprising and gave her hope that her wedding and marriage could mend the old rivalry between the Bisset and Williams families. Finally she was getting the life she wanted where her name was in the press for a positive reason and not because of scandal.

Nine

Iris wasn't sure how to act when Zac arrived in the suite. She'd been dressed and ready for more than thirty minutes, in fact, since he'd texted her that he was getting close. Now she was hovering in the main living area while he was settling into the smaller room in the suite and getting dressed for dinner.

"I'm ready," he said.

She swallowed hard when she saw him. He wore a pair of shorts, deck shoes and a button-down shirt. His blond hair was tousled as if he'd run his hands through it. Her own fingers tingled as she remembered how soft and thick his hair was and how it had felt to hold his head to her breast while they'd been making love.

She shook her head. *Stop it.* She needed to stay

focused. This was the second test of her and Zac as a believable couple.

"Do I look okay?" he asked. "You're kind of staring at me…"

"You look fine. I was just thinking about something else," she said. Yeah, like how good he had looked naked. "So, Adler and Nick are two of my oldest friends. They will be subtle but they're going to dig and try to find out when we started dating and everything."

"So, it's dinner with the family, part two," he said with a chuckle. "Don't worry, angel face, Adler's my family as well so I know how to handle her."

Angel face.

It was a sweet endearment. To be honest, she'd never had one in a relationship before unless *babe* counted. But she'd never felt it had.

"Crapola. I didn't want to tell her in a text and we didn't end up meeting in person this afternoon. She's going to have all kinds of questions. This is a bad idea," she said abruptly. She hadn't really given much thought to the fact that Adler was Zac's cousin. That might make things complicated down the road. As if sleeping with a guy she had hired wasn't already a bad idea. This was what happened when she let Thea get in her head. She started making decisions from a place of panic instead of a place of reason.

Zac came over and put his arms around her, hugging her close and then stepping back. "Relax. Whatever happens, we will roll with it. We're still new to the relationship… By the way, my family is going to be grilling you and probably trying to figure out what you see in me."

"Why would they do that?" she asked.

"I'm pretty much always focused on yacht designs, team dynamics and how to win the America's Cup. I'm told I can be boring AF when I get on a roll about it," he said. "So there is that. I know that we have a contract for me to be here, but I genuinely like you, Iris. I think if we just are honest about our reactions to each other, throw in a few kisses and longing glances, no one will be suspicious."

She stared up into his bright blue eyes and nodded. He made it sound so simple, but she knew that it was way more complex than that. She took his hand in hers. He had some callouses, probably owing to a lifetime spent working on boats, but she liked the way he immediately squeezed her hand.

"I like you too," she admitted.

"I already knew that," he said with a cheeky grin as he led them out of the suite.

He started down the hall, but she stayed to watch the door close and then double-checked the handle. He stopped, arching one eyebrow at her in question.

"Sorry, habit," she said.

"That's a good one," he said.

Graham had hated that she did it and said it made her look like a paranoid weirdo. But then she was coming to realize that a lot of the things Graham had said about her weren't a reflection of her but rather of him. As much as she'd been trying to find the perfect mate, he'd been trying to find a woman who fit what he wanted. A woman Iris realized she hadn't ever been nor truly wanted to be. And that was okay.

Zac came back and double-checked the door as well before taking her hand and walking toward the elevators. He had his faults; she knew he did. No one was perfect—man or woman—but there were a lot of qualities to Zac that she'd never realized mattered to her before. And she knew that it wasn't the qualities per se but Zac himself.

There was an elderly couple on the elevator holding hands when they got on and they smiled at the two of them. For a moment—just the briefest second—Iris saw herself and Zac in them, but she knew that was an illusion and warned herself not to buy into it.

He had said they were friends and could make this work for the weekend. He hadn't said anything about beyond that. He was here for the time being and she had to remember that he was going to leave once his funding came in and this destination-wedding weekend ended they would start to "drift" apart and their relationship would end in three months' time. So these four days were really all they'd have together.

The lobby was crowded with people as they exited the elevator and walked toward the hotel entrance. There was a pianist playing Gershwin and the buzz of muted conversations filled the room. Iris heard a woman's laugh and turned to see Adler and Nick talking to Nick's mother, Cora. The threesome looked happy as they were talking. Adler glanced up and noticed Iris and waved, then did a double take at Zac.

She shook her head as she started walking over to them.

"Girl, why didn't you tell me your new man was my cousin?" Adler said, hugging her and then reaching over to hug Zac.

"I told her I wanted to surprise you. I wasn't supposed to be here until tomorrow," Zac said effortlessly.

Taking all the pressure off Iris for not saying anything. Adler hugged her close and Iris actually relaxed for a moment.

"He's way better than Graham," Adler whispered in her ear before turning back to Zac. "This is a very good surprise! Come meet Nick and his mom."

"I can't wait," Zac said.

Adler led the way toward them, and Zac kept his hand firmly in hers, bringing her along with him and making it clear they were together.

Adler hadn't seen Zac in person for five years. He had signed a three-year contract with an America's Cup team and had spent the time racing and training. She didn't know the details but her tall blond cousin had fallen out with the captain and hadn't renewed his contract. For as long as she'd known Zac, yachting was his life, so it was interesting to see him holding Iris's hand and laughing at her story of how she'd botched her family's famous lobster roll recipe on the morning show two weeks earlier.

Something seemed…too perfect, too right be-tween Iris and Zac. Adler knew she should just smile and go along with it, but she didn't want to see her friend get hurt.

The thing was, Iris looked vulnerable sitting next to Zac. She smiled when he looked over at her but when he wasn't looking, her friend was staring at him like she was…well, like she really cared for him. Something Adler had never seen Iris do when she'd been with Graham.

Nick pinched her leg under the table and she glared at him. He leaned in to kiss her neck and whispered in her ear, "Stop staring at them. It's clear you're not buying them as a couple."

"What are you two talking about?" Iris asked. "When they kiss like that, they're giving each other the low-down."

Exactly, Adler thought. Iris would know she'd pick up on whatever was going on.

The downside to having been best friends for all of their adult lives was that Adler and Iris knew each other's little social tells.

"Nothing important. I need to powder my nose. Want to join me?" Adler said, jumping up.

"You're not wearing—" Nick said, but stopped when Adler turned to face him, raising both eye-brows. He'd probably been about to point out she wasn't wearing makeup, which her wedding skin-care consultant had advised for a few days before the ceremony so she'd be picture-perfect on the big day.

"I'd love to," Iris said with a giggle. "Be right back."

Iris squeezed Zac's shoulder, started to walk away and then turned back to kiss him. It seemed like she was aiming for his cheek, but he turned into the kiss and their lips met. The kiss was the first convincing moment for Adler when she totally bought them as a couple.

Was it just new couple awkwardness?

She glanced at Nick, who smiled and shrugged at her. He seemed to be thinking the same thing. But she'd get to the bottom of it in the bathroom.

Iris's skin was flushed as she brushed past Adler and led the way to the bathroom at the back of the restaurant. Adler followed her friend, knowing that she should have insisted they talk today before the men had arrived. But with her wedding planner, Jaqs Veerland, flying in midday to go over last-minute details, she hadn't had time.

"Okay, spill," Adler said once they were in the ladies' room.

"Spill what?"

"The tea, girl. And don't pretend there isn't any. You and Zac…you almost make sense but something isn't feeling right."

Iris fumbled in her purse for her lip gloss and turned to the mirror. "I'm sure I don't know what you mean."

"I'm sure you do," Adler said, swiping the gloss from Iris and putting on some herself. "That kiss looked real but the rest of it…you were watching him like you weren't sure about him. What's going on?"

Iris shrugged and took the lip gloss back. "I wish I had your skin. You're glowing."

"Thanks. But I'm not going to let you distract me."

"There's nothing to tell. He's hot and we had this zing… I mean, I almost fell and he caught me and kissed me and the paparazzi went crazy snapping photos and it's just sort of gone on from there. We are still in the very beginning of this relationship. Remember when you wouldn't eat in front of Nick?"

Adler did remember. She'd liked him so much she hadn't wanted to do anything to put him off. A previous dude she'd dated had said her chewing was too loud, so she hadn't been able to eat in front of Nick.

"Fair point. I just worry about you, Iris," Adler said.

"I know," Iris responded, wrapping her arms around Adler's shoulders as the two of them stared at their reflection in the mirror. "I love you for that."

Adler reached up and patted Iris's hands. "Nick is never going to let me live this down. He said I was staring at you both like I wanted to do an interrogation."

"You were," Iris admitted. "Which wasn't helping my nerves. Do you like him?"

"Zac?"

"Yes."

"I do. When we were kids, he was always outside on the water. And he could always be counted on to help me disappear when I needed some breathing room by taking me sailing. He's not much of a talker, but that was when we were kids. He pretty much is always away sailing now. How is this going to work?"

"We haven't figured that part out," Iris said. "Right now, we are both here and enjoying each other's company."

"And you'd appreciate it if I let you do that, right?"

"Yes," Iris said. "Also, this is your big week. We should all be thinking about you."

"You should," Adler said with a wink. "I have my final fitting tomorrow after the family luncheon. Will you go with me?"

"Yes. I'm all yours. I'm filming a segment early in the morning. I heard your dad wrote a new song for you."

"Yeah, he did," Adler said. "He's been more... sentimental since the heart attack. He won't let me hear it before my wedding day."

They rejoined the men and Adler was satisfied her friend was going to be okay, which meant she was back to worrying about how her Uncle Auggie was going to be tomorrow when he was in the same room with his most hated rival, Tad Williams—Nick's dad.

"So, you're the America's Cup guy?" Nick asked as the ladies left the table.

Zac reached for his water glass and nodded. "You're the...titan of industry, right?"

Nick gave a shout of laughter. "I'm guessing that's

what Adler said. I know for damn sure your father and brother don't call me that."

"No, they usually throw in some derogatory curse words," Zac allowed. Nick was a really nice guy and it was clear to Zac that Nick truly loved Adler. Zac saw real affection between them. Having grown up with parents who had been in and out of love with each other several times, Zac knew how rare that kind of bond was.

"I do the same when referring to them. I'm trying to make peace for Adler's sake," Nick said. "I was surprised by the invitation to your grandmother's for lunch tomorrow."

"Me too," Zac admitted. "I don't think my dad is mellowing, he just knows there will be hell to pay if he upsets Adler. She's my mom's only connection to her sister and she is pulling out all the stops to make the wedding is everything that Adler wants."

"I know. It's so crazy. I like your mom, by the way. She's sweet and funny," he said. "Makes me wonder how she raised a shark like Logan."

"Fair enough, but I think Logan was always Dad's shadow, not Mom's, so that might be one explanation. He's a great guy away from the office," Zac said. He and his siblings were very close, but he was realistic enough to know that they had both good and bad qualities. "We're all very driven."

"I've seen that. What's going on with your America's Cup team? I heard a rumor that you're looking for financing," Nick said.

"I'm not," Zac said. Using the Collins connection

to finance his bid was one thing, accepting financing from his families' business rivals would put Zac in direct confrontation with his father and Logan. Something that Zac wasn't interested in doing. He wanted to do this on his own; he had never been looking to piss off his family.

"Okay, but if that changes, I'm interested," Nick said.

"Dude, you know that I can't even contemplate doing business with you," Zac said. "I might spend most of my time on a yacht but if I accepted an investment from you, I'd never be able to come home again. As sweet as my mom has been to you, she'd be royally ticked at the both of us, and let me tell you, that isn't a good thing to be on the receiving end of."

Nick put his hands up. "Gotcha. I'm just always looking for new investments."

"And if it happens to piss off the Bissets, all the better?" Zac asked.

"Sometimes, but honestly that's more my dad's thing than mine. I go after sound investments, not just things I think August Bisset wants," Nick said.

"So you didn't start dating Adler because she's related to my mom?" Zac asked.

"Not at all. She's not a Bisset, which of course is a plus in my opinion, but also I don't spend all of my time trying to undermine your family," he said, leaning back in his chair, glass in hand. "Whatever happened between our fathers happened way before I was born and to be honest it doesn't bother me."

"Glad to hear it. I'm sure Logan wouldn't agree."

"Logan's a douche," Nick said. "He's gone straight after some of my business, but I don't mind a good honest fight."

"Who's fighting?" Adler asked, sitting back down.

"No one tonight," Nick said. "And I promised to be nice tomorrow so we should be good."

Zac hoped they would be. Iris seemed different when she sat back down, not so smiley as she'd been before. Had Adler figured out what they were up to?

But when he glanced at his cousin, she just winked at him so he didn't think she'd found out about their arrangement. He reached for Iris's hand as the check arrived, but she moved away from him, taking the check from the waiter. "This one is on me. Thanks for making time for a quiet meal during your special week."

"Any time, Iris," Adler said.

Zac took the check from her. "Sorry, angel face, but I'll get this."

She glared at him. He guessed that she expected her fake boyfriend to stay quiet and let her pay, but he hadn't been raised that way. And though he knew she made damn good money, there was no way he could tamp down this impulse.

"Angel face?"

"Shut it, Addie. I'm sure Nick has a special name for you," Zac said.

"Does he?" Iris asked as Zac took his American Express from his wallet and handed it to the waiter.

"I do," Nick said. "But I've been warned to keep it behind closed doors."

"Oooh, what is it?" Iris asked. "Now I'm dying to know."

"Stop it," Adler said. "If you were really my friend, you wouldn't want to know."

"Is it embarrassing?" Iris asked. "It can't be. You're too adorable to have a nickname that's not cool."

"It's private," Adler said.

"Fair enough."

Zac smiled at his cousin, who had spent so much of her life in the spotlight. It was nice to know she had someone in her life who would keep her secrets and share things just with her.

Until that moment Zac hadn't realized that there was such a thing. His parents presented a united front for show, but he'd never seen them as a couple in love. And, honestly, that hadn't been something he'd thought he'd wanted in his life until Iris slipped her hand in his and squeezed it.

Ten

A walk on the beach. It was simple. It was romantic. It was expected. Iris told herself that as she slipped her hand into Zac's and followed him down the wooden boardwalk to the shore. In the distance she heard the sound of waves and she stopped for a moment, tipping her head back to look up at the black sky and breathe in the salty air.

Zac just stood next to her, letting her have her moment. She forgot how to breathe sometimes. Not like the normal inhale/exhale thing, but how to take these moments and press them into her mind so she wouldn't forget them.

And she wanted to remember this night with Zac. He'd been funny and charming at dinner—the perfect companion. How had she never noticed that Graham only talked about himself? Zac was the total opposite, asking questions and genuinely listening when everyone spoke.

If she'd had to invent an ideal man for herself, so far he was ticking all of the boxes. The cynical part of her mind warned that he was ticking them because she'd paid him to be by her side. It was a little too convenient.

"You okay?" he asked.

"Yeah," she said, wrapping one arm around her own waist as she dropped his hand. "Why?"

"You looked so relaxed and chill. And then I don't know what happened in that pretty head of yours but you started to look stressed."

She shook her head. "I don't know what happened either. Thea says I overthink everything. She might be right."

Zac reached for her hand and she let him take it. "When I first started sailing, I had a mentor who told me that there were a million things that needed to happen and could go wrong while I was on the water. He said just take each moment as it comes, the strong wind that fills your sails, the spray of water on your face, the storm that blows up out of nowhere. Each moment. That's all you can handle and all you can control."

She knew that. She did. But it was harder to do than Zac made it sound. "I try. Somehow the future always tugs at me, making me anxious to plan for it."

He laughed. "I can see that. I struggle with it as

well but then I like finding a solution or a work-around. Want me to help you figure this out?"

She shook her head. "I don't know how to work around you."

"Me?"

"Yes, you. You're not at all what I thought you'd be," she said. "You've been surprising me every step of the way and that keeps making me think things that—"

"Stop," he said, tugging her gently into his arms. "Don't do that. I told you we'd be honest with each other. The way we started out doesn't have to define every moment."

She looked up at him. The lights from the board-walk were dim where they stood and his blue eyes were dark. He'd shaved before he'd come to Nantucket. He looked casual, but his jaw was strong, and she couldn't help letting her eyes fall to his lips.

Those lips that she'd kissed last night. Those lips that had charted a path down her body and left her quivering in his arms. She wanted to taste him again. To pretend that they were like Nick and Adler sneaking away to be alone and enjoy the simple romance of an evening at the beach.

She put her hand on the back of his neck as she went up on tiptoe, mesmerized by the thought of that kiss. He tipped his head to the side and she came closer. The warmth of his breath brushed over her mouth as he exhaled. She closed her eyes and his lips touched hers. A shiver went down her spine and she tightened her fingers on the back of his neck.

Swallowing hard as he lifted his head, he stared down into her face. Their eyes met, and she felt like…she wanted to believe that something magical passed between them. Something that would bind them together as a couple. But the truth was she was searching for that connection and she didn't trust her chronic bad taste when it came to men. Didn't trust her gut when it shouted to take him back to the room and make love to him all night.

She wanted to believe she could keep her wits about her, but she knew she couldn't. She was lying to her best friend, lying to her parents and her sister. The one person she couldn't lie to was herself.

She wouldn't be that girl who fell for a pair of blue eyes that promised the moon and woke up in the sand underneath a cloudy sky.

She took a deeper breath as she stepped back. "I think I've had enough of the night air. I'm going to head back to the room."

"Running away from me isn't going to change anything," he said.

She wanted to pretend not to understand what he meant but she wasn't going to play games with him either. "I know that. But I need bright lights and re-ality instead of this."

"This?"

"This…" She gestured to the sky and the beach and him. "I'm not living a picture-perfect moment that I'm going to share with my followers. This isn't real. Any of it. And I don't want to forget it."

She pivoted on her heel and walked away from

him. It was hard, but she knew in the moment that it was what she needed to do. She had to stay focused or she was going to lose control of more than her emotions. She was going to lose control of her life and everything she'd worked for would be gone.

Zac knew he should let her go. She'd been pretty damn plain when she'd said this was an illusion. But he wasn't faking it. He liked her. He wanted her. He followed her, putting his hand on her shoulder to stop her.

"What?" she asked, her tone short and curt.

"You forgot one thing, angel face," he said. "I'm real. You're real. And neither one of us is lying about that."

She chewed her lower lip and he remembered the last time she'd done that: when they'd made love the first time. He was no closer now to figuring out what was going on inside her head than he had been that night. And true, it had only been a week earlier, but it felt like they'd spent a lifetime together since then. He hadn't wanted to believe that he'd ever feel like this about a woman…especially not one that he'd made a deal to date.

He hoped he wasn't. And this wasn't love, was it? Could it be?

It was lust. He was even comfortable labeling it affection and/or infatuation. But beyond that, the answer had to be no. They were in a business arrangement and only a fool would allow it to become too emotional. And despite what his brothers sometimes said Zac wasn't anyone's fool.

"I'm not calling you a liar," she said at last. Her tone was serious and grounded, the kind of tone she'd used when she'd been meeting with her fans earlier in the lobby.

He didn't say anything because he'd noticed that at times she would drop a leading statement and see how he responded. But he wasn't sure what to say to her now.

"I'm talking about myself," she said at last. "We have a contracted agreement and I know what I wanted from it. But here in the moonlight, holding your hand and just standing next to you, I guess I wish we didn't have that. That we were just two people…"

He had thought that, as well. "Would you have spoken to me if you hadn't needed me?"

She shrugged. But they both knew the answer was no. She wasn't at the point in her life where she really wanted a man in it. He was starting to realize that. She liked him and he liked her but it was in spite of their agreement. Neither of them was ready for a serious relationship. He was leaving to train for the America's Cup and she was launching a new line for her brand.

This pact they'd made for Adler's wedding, that was all they had and neither of them should forget it.

"No," she said at last.

"Me neither."

"Why not?"

"You're complicated, angel face," he said.

"So?"

"I like it, you know I do, but the truth is, we're here together because of some very unique circumstances."

"So talking about what-ifs isn't going to work," she said. "I just feel myself wanting to believe this is real in my heart and my mind is warning me that it isn't."

He pulled her into his arms because he hated not touching her when they were this close, and he was tired of denying himself and letting her set the pace. "This is real, Iris. It's just going to end when the weekend is over and we start drifting apart over the next three months. That doesn't mean we won't feel something for each other. I think it would be odd if we didn't. All it really means is that we might look back and wish it had lasted longer..."

He wanted to add that there was no reason it couldn't but that was more complicated than he wanted to be tonight. The wind was blowing off the water and the salt air was making him long to be back out on the deck of his yacht, challenging the elements and competing for his place in history.

But...

He also wanted Iris. He wanted to keep her in his arms and hold on to her until the winds and time forced him to leave her. That was something he knew he couldn't really have.

As much as he wanted to hold her in his moment, when the sea called, he'd answer. Winning the America's Cup with his own team had long been a dream of his. Something he needed to do to prove himself, to show his old man what he was capable of.

She reached up and touched his face. There was a hint of sadness to her smile and he knew she had come to the same realization that he had. No matter how much they both might want to believe that they should have more with each other, the contract they'd signed was all that either of them was willing to give.

He'd thought of her as a siren leading him astray, but he realized that he didn't want to disappoint Iris. He needed to be his best self and that meant that he couldn't detour from his chosen path because she wouldn't detour from hers.

She needed him to be the man she'd met. The man who was a sailor and a competitor and whose life was on the sea. Not in Boston or wherever her career took her.

He leaned down to kiss her because he knew that these four days were really the most intimate time they would have together, and the pipe dream of more time was hard to let go. But in his heart and soul, he knew that was the only option. He'd taken her up on her indecent proposal never guessing that he would ever feel anything this strong for her or that the thought of leaving her would cut like a knife.

She wrapped her arms around his shoulders, and he knew that no matter what, he wasn't going to be able to stop himself from making love to her over the next four days. They might both know that their relationship would end but he needed to give them enough memories to keep them company over the long dark nights that lay ahead.

She wanted to pretend it was a fluke, that their one night together hadn't changed her forever but she knew it had. Sitting at the table with Adler and Nick tonight had just driven home to her how much she wanted everything about her and Zac to be real. She didn't want it to be just for the weekend and just for show. He'd been funny and charming and just so damn real that it had driven home how wrong her search for a partner had gone up until that point.

He complemented her in a way no one else ever had. A part of her knew it had to be because she wasn't trying to impress him. She knew he wasn't going to leave her alone in a hotel room the way that Graham had. She was paying him to be with her.

God. How humiliating would it be if that ever got out? But she had no regrets. Being with Zac had shown her a side of herself she hadn't even realized she'd been burying.

It was hard to realize what was missing until she'd found it. She pulled back from the kiss but didn't want to. She liked the way he tasted and it felt as if it had been years instead of a week since they'd kissed.

He kept his hands around her waist. When he turned to shelter her from the wind, she again felt her heart melt just the tiniest bit. He held her as if she were precious to him and she realized that despite the fact that she ran a multimillion-dollar company and she could hold her own with anyone on the planet, it was nice to have someone hold her and shelter her.

She reached up to touch his face, felt the light stubble that was starting to grow on his jaw. In his eyes, she thought she saw the same heaviness that troubled her.

"I know I said no sex, but would you be upset if I changed my mind?" she asked.

He threw his head back and laughed, and she couldn't help smiling. She loved the sound of his laughter. He held nothing back when he did it.

"Uh, no, angel face, I wouldn't mind at all. In fact, I think I'd be downright ticked if you didn't."

"Good. I mean you did say there wasn't anything I could ask you to do that would make you uncomfortable."

"There's something in your tone that's making me think I shouldn't have issued a blanket challenge to you like that," he said.

"You shouldn't have," she quipped but she knew he was safe. She wanted him to herself but would never do anything that would make him feel ill at ease. He had given her a freedom she hadn't realized she'd denied herself. And it was making her regret that she'd waited so long to find it.

She'd never thought sexual confidence was something she needed in her life. But since being with Zac that one night, she was already a different woman. She wanted to see what happened if they made love twice.

How would that change her?

She was ready for it.

"This is our last night before everyone is here," she said. "Our last night as a quasi-anonymous couple. What should we do?"

"Something daring and not in the rule book?" he asked.

She took a deep breath. She wasn't worried about his suggesting a three-way the way Graham had or that she wear a dildo and take him from behind. That wasn't the kind of man Zac was. In fact, she was excited to hear what he suggested.

"Yes."

"Hmm… Want to take my grandmother's yacht out and make love on the deck with just the sea around us and the moon and stars watching overhead?"

She inhaled sharply, already picturing him nude on the deck of a yacht. She was the tiniest bit afraid of water… But they wouldn't be in the water, and the chance to be the woman with him on the yacht— sharing his world—was too powerful to resist.

"Okay. Let's do it."

He took her hand in his and led the way back up the beach toward the marina. He talked to her as they walked, telling her about his earliest memories of sailing. "It was my gran who first took me out on the ocean and let me get behind the wheel. She taught me about the jib and the wind and how to harness it. She made it seem okay that when my father bellowed and yelled, I ran and hid."

Iris caught her breath as he talked about his childhood. She'd heard from Adler that August Bisset wasn't an easy man to live with. Adler rarely saw her uncle, but Zac had grown up underneath his roof and his upbringing was so different from Iris's. So foreign. Her parents had wanted them to achieve but nothing had been more important to them than making sure that she and her sister were loved.

Something that Iris realized she'd taken for granted.

She stopped Zac when they were on the slip about to board his grandmother's yacht, the Day Dream.

"Changed your mind?" he asked.

"Not at all," she said, hugging him and pulling him closer to her so she could whisper in his ear. "Thank you for being you."

He squeezed her close for a long minute and then let his arms fall to his sides. He didn't respond and she hadn't expected him to. She knew how hard it was to live with someone so demanding, and the fact that Zac had made the relationship with his father work by going his own way was more impressive than he knew. He hadn't chosen the easy path; he'd moved halfway around the world and started over. He thought he was a man who always looked for the horizon because he was running but she knew now that he did that because he was harnessing the bluster he'd inherited from his father and charting his own course.

She wished she could chart a course that would keep her by his side and didn't even care if that made her seem weak. She liked him and she wanted to keep him in her life but she had no idea if that was something that was even possible.

Eleven

Piloting the small yacht out of the marina at night was as familiar to him as the back of his hand. Once he'd gotten them out into Nantucket Sound, Iris stood in his arms at the helm of the boat. He steered them far away from the lights of Nantucket until it felt like they were the only two people left on earth.

And knowing that tomorrow he'd be surrounded by his family and there would be all of the activities of Adler's wedding party, he wanted to make this night last forever. As much as he prided himself on being the anti-Bisset Bisset he knew once he was with his brothers and sister that he'd fall back into the role that he always played with them and, of course, he had the added role of being Iris's boyfriend for the weekend.

But tonight they were Zac and Iris. "I almost wish we were living in a different time. I'd spirit you away on the high seas and we'd stop wherever we hit land, and no one would know who we were."

"You'd run away with me?"

"Hell, yes. Would you?"

She thought about it too long and he knew the answer was no, no matter what she said. Of course, Iris wouldn't run away. She wasn't about running away. She was about making a plan and then following it until its end. No matter what.

"I'm kidding," he said. "The sea just calls to me."

But it was too late to pull back that feeling even though he'd tried to cover it. He'd always know he'd thrown out something that was real and she'd drawn back. He reminded himself that she was a very attractive woman who had decided to hire a man for the weekend instead of finding a real boyfriend.

His thoughts were ruining the night. He needed tonight to be a happy memory for both of them, but maybe it was Nantucket or just thinking about his family that had soured him.

"I'm sorry," she said. "I want to say yes, but I'd be so freaked out about not knowing where we were going and not having a plan that I'd make you miserable. Do I want to be with you…?"

She stopped talking and turned in his arms as he hit the anchor release button and was about to turn away from her. She put her arms around his waist and rested her head on his chest right over his heart.

"More than anything," she said. Her voice was low, but he still heard her.

"Then why do you hesitate?"

"I'm afraid," she said, then let out a deep breath that sounded like a sigh. "I can only let my guard down because I know whatever I do you're not going to leave me. And if we started really dating, I'd let the pressure of that expectation overwhelm me. I know that makes me sound shallow."

"No," he said. "It doesn't. It makes you human, angel face."

She looked up at him then and he didn't care that she knew he wanted to run away with her. He could make whatever excuses he wanted to, he was going to miss the hell out of her when their arrangement was over and he started his training for the America's Cup. He'd go because that was his life, but he'd always look back to this moment and this night with her.

"Want to skinny dip?" he asked, because if he didn't do something, he was going to say all kinds of things that would scare her so much it would send her swimming back to shore.

"I'm afraid of the water."

"I'll protect you," he said. "But no pressure if you don't want to go in."

She chewed her lower lip. "How about if you skinny dip and I stand on the deck and watch?"

"Will you be naked?" he asked.

"I could be," she said. "Seems only fair if one of us is going to strip down, we both should."

"It does," he said, trying not to let himself fall a little bit more for her. There was so much daring inside her but she was afraid to let it out except in little controlled bursts. And he had to admit that made her all the more attractive.

He took her hand and led her to the deck of the yacht, then waggled his eyebrows at her as he took off his shirt and then his pants. He stood in front of her in his boxer briefs and put his hands on his hips. "One of us is a bit ahead of the other one."

"One of us is just wearing a thong under their dress," she said, untying the halter neck and letting the dress fall from her.

His breath caught in his throat as he stared at her beautiful nearly naked body. She stood there in the light of the full moon and the illumination provided by the running lights and reached up to undo the clasp that held her hair back. Her hair spilled down over her shoulders and she lifted her arms as the gentle summer breeze blew around them.

It should have cooled him off but even an Arctic breeze wouldn't have lessened the heat she stirred in him. He was hot and hard and at the same time he wanted to cuddle her in his arms and just keep her safe. He wished the world could see this Iris. The one with her arms in the air, bare breasts uplifted and a huge-ass smile on her face. Gone were her barriers and the proper behavior she used to keep the world at arm's length.

"God, you're gorgeous," he said. His words were low and rumbling but that was all he could manage.

She tipped her head to the side and smiled at him. "I want to point out all the places I'm not, but I can see you think I am, so I'll keep it to myself."

"I'm glad because I wasn't just talking about your body. There's something about you, Iris, that I can't resist."

Zac made her feel different and she wasn't sure she wanted to resist it. She let her arms fall to her sides and stood more fully facing him. He was turned on by her—that was easy to see—but there was a lot more than sexy times between them.

He'd asked her to run away with him and she'd panicked. Not because she didn't want to but because, for a split second, she wished she was the kind of woman who would. But she knew that the contract had freed something inside of her. It was novel and new, and she was enjoying it because it was shocking her to her staid core. But if that was her norm, she didn't think she'd enjoy it as much.

And she knew he would. She didn't want to hurt Zac. Heck, she'd been hurt too many times by relationships to want to risk another one—hence, the contract.

"Are you still feeling like a swim?" she asked, coming closer to him. She loved his body and honestly it would be perfectly okay with her if he were naked 24/7 when they were alone together. He had been sweet to compliment her but he had the kind of body that would make anyone stop and stare.

"Well, not exactly," he said, reaching out to cup

one of her breasts in his hand. He rubbed his thumb over her nipple, and it beaded under his touch.

Remembering the scar she'd felt the first time they'd made love, she reached out and touched it again. She leaned in closer and saw it was jagged and still had some redness around it. "What is this from?"

"Stupidity," he said.

"I've done a lot of stupid things but don't have a scar like this," she said, tracing the edges of it with a gentle finger, wishing she could have soothed the hurt it must have caused him.

"Well, when you combine alcohol with ego and a competitive nature, this is the result. I did a kite-surfing challenge with a teammate, won, celebrated too vigorously and ended up crashing into an out-cropping of rocks I hadn't noticed."

"That does sound…"

"Dumb. You can say it. My mom and sister both said it was what I deserved. Apparently, my victory dances are a little OTT."

She had to laugh at the way he said it, but her laughter turned to sensual awareness as his hand moved from her breast to her waist and he drew her closer to him. Her naked breasts were cushioned against his upper body. His chest hair was soft against her skin and his heat was a contrast to the breeze blowing around them. He smelled of his aftershave—a clean, crisp scent—and the sea breeze. She closed her eyes and willed her mind to stop thinking. To just relax and enjoy this. But she wanted to record every second.

Her life had been played out on TV and on social media since she'd entered college. By her own design, of course, but so many of her ups and downs had been recorded and scrutinized on the gossip websites that she almost didn't believe her own reality until she saw it played back. Until she flipped past her profile and saw that smiling face.

She knew she was here with him. She wanted to just enjoy him but—

"Stop thinking," he said. "It's disconcerting to watch you go from enjoying my touch to suddenly seeming to analyze everything."

Busted.

"Damn. I'm sorry. I'm such a freak about things like that. I don't know what my deal—"

He stopped the stream of words with a kiss. She stopped thinking, stopped worrying and calculating her responses. She just clung to his shoulders as his tongue rubbed over hers and his hands splayed warm and wide on her back. She arched into the curve of his body and felt his erection pushing against her. She flexed her fingers against his skin and couldn't help the groan that started deep inside her as her entire body seemed to start pulsing in time with her heartbeat. She wanted this.

She wanted him.

And she wasn't going to allow her own self-consciousness to stop her from enjoying this.

She ran her hand down his arm, felt the flex of his

biceps and squeezed them. She loved his strength. Loved how easily he held her and yet how gently he did it. He was aware of his strength and never used it to overwhelm her even though he easily could. He broke their kiss, his mouth moving down the column of her neck, biting gently at the junction where it sloped into her collarbone.

She caressed his chest, flexing her fingers and letting her nails scrape over his skin. He shuddered at her touch and she continued to move her hand down his body. But he stopped her, turning her in his arms and pulling her close against his chest. His erection nestled between her buttocks and he put one hand on her stomach and the other between her legs.

She rocked her hips back against him and he brought his hand up to her chin, tipping her head back and to the side to kiss her again. His mouth was warm and wet, drawing her deeper into the sensual web he was weaving around them. She felt his finger move under the fabric of her underwear to the juncture of her thighs. She reached back between their bodies, fondling him through his boxer briefs, realizing that the only thought she had was how to get him inside of her.

Iris felt so good in his arms that he wanted the moment to never end but he also needed to be inside of her. To take her and pretend that this night could last forever. He pushed her thong down her legs, and she kicked them aside as she turned in his arms and he shoved his underwear off so that her hand was on his naked shaft. He continued kissing her as he walked her backward to the soft cushions on the deck near the railing. He lifted his head for a moment, trying to gauge how quickly he could get to the cushions and get inside of her but she pushed him back on the padded bench and straddled him as she had for a few moments the first time they'd made love.

"I want to be on top the entire time," she said. "I feel like I let you take control from the very first moment and this time it's all me."

"Yes, ma'am," he said. "I've got a condom in my pants pocket."

"Stay right there," she said.

He did as she ordered, watching her walk across the deck to where he'd dropped his trousers. She bent over and as she did, glanced back at him and realized he was watching her. She stopped just like that, her beautiful backside pointed at him, her hair hanging down as she smiled back at him. She took the condom from his pocket and then slowly stood back up, turning to face him.

He was stroking his cock as he watched her, and this time when she walked toward him, her gait was deliberate and her intent was to turn him on. Her full breasts bounced with her steps and her hips swayed. She was taking control of not just their lovemaking but of the night.

He felt like he was going burst as she stopped in front of him and dropped to her knees. Leaning forward, she stroked her tongue along the side of his shaft before taking him into her mouth. His hips jerked forward and he put his hand on the back of her head, touching her briefly before moving his hand away. She reached between them, stroking his shaft while she continued to suck on the tip. He felt like he was going to come in her mouth and that was the last thing he wanted for this night. He shifted his hips and went down on his knees next to her on the deck, taking the condom from her hand and quickly sheathing himself with it. He turned her around so she was facing the ocean, then took one of her hands and put it on the bench underneath his.

He put his other hand on her stomach, pushed her hips back toward him and entered her from behind. She moaned and turned her hand over underneath his, twining their fingers together, her hips rocking back against him as he entered her deeper. He palmed her breast with his free hand and kissed the side of her neck. She threw her head back as he started to pump his hips and drove himself into her again and again.

She turned her head and he found her mouth with his. He was totally in tune with her as they both ground harder and harder against each other until he felt himself about to come. But he wasn't sure she was with him. He reached between her legs, flicking her clit with his finger, rubbing it the way she'd liked it the other night. She ripped her mouth from his, threw back her head and screamed his name.

He held her hips with both hands, thrusting into her one more time, harder and deeper than before. But it wasn't enough. He drew back and drove himself into her again and again until his release washed over him and he collapsed forward, putting his hand on the bench to make sure he didn't crush her. She wrapped her hand around his wrist, her breath sawing in and out of her body.

He lifted himself from her, pulled her to her feet and then sat down on the bench and cuddled her in his lap. She looked as dazed as he felt. He was totally sated from their lovemaking. She'd done something to him. Snapped that control he'd always relied on to keep his wits about him and make sure he didn't dive in to deep.

But he knew he had. As she curled up on his lap, putting her head on his shoulder and wrapping her arms around him, all he could do was stroke her back and remind himself that he was a man who loved the next horizon more than anything on shore, even though at this moment, with the moon shining down on them, it felt like a lie.

He knew he should say something or get up and start steering them back to Nantucket. But he didn't want this moment to end. She didn't say anything either, just held on to him. He felt like they both knew that something had changed between them.

He thought he might be overthinking it, but he couldn't deny the truth that he felt deep in his soul. Iris Collins was changing him, and he was half addicted to it, half resentful of it. His life had worked for so long because he'd found his place and his way of coping with it. He wasn't sure he was ready to change for her or for anyone else.

And he damned sure knew he didn't want to go into this weekend feeling like this. He needed to be his strongest self, not whatever this was that making love to Iris had made him.

Twelve

Iris had woken up in Zac's arms at 4:00 a.m. in a total panic. She didn't want to dwell on the night before. The moonlight, the ocean, the man.

She was losing control of herself and of the situation with Zac. Last night had changed something inside of her and she didn't like it. She wasn't about to give up on everything she'd worked for because she had a lover who knew how to please her for the first time in her life. And she was ashamed of boiling Zac's good qualities down to the fact that he knew how to make her orgasm, but that was how she was going to cope with him.

She had gotten out of bed at seven o'clock and snuck into the bathroom to change into her exercise clothes. She'd only packed them for lounging in her room, but she needed to get out of the hotel and away from Zac. She needed to think and put everything in perspective.

She had wedding fever, she thought as she started out on a slow jog down the path toward the beach. But she hated running and as soon as she was out of sight of the hotel, slowed to a walk. She wished her walk would bring her a solution to what she should do. But she'd really made a mess of things this time. It would have been easier if she'd just had Zac show up on the day of the event and look pretty on her arm. But no, she'd found a guy who knew the bride and who was…well, more than Iris had expected him to be.

He was complicating her well-ordered life and she wasn't too sure she liked it.

"Iris?"

She glanced over her shoulder to see Juliette Bisset. "Hi, Mrs. B. What are you doing out here so early?"

"Same as you, I imagine," Juliette said.

God, Iris really hoped not. "I guess hosting your husband's rivals at your mom's house would be a little bit stressful."

Juliette smiled and shook her head. "You have no idea. I've never met Nick's family because…well, Tad and Cora didn't want to meet me. But I'm glad that August is making the effort for Adler. The last thing a new bride needs is tension in her marriage."

It sounded like Mrs. B was speaking from experience. Iris wanted to know more—she couldn't help it—but manners and breeding kept her from asking. "That's true of any relationship."

"I heard you're dating my son," Juliette said.

"I am," Iris said, not sure what Zac had told his mom about them. "It happened kind of quick."

"That's what Zac said," Juliette said. "I'm not going to pry or anything. Just wanted to say I like the idea of you and Zac together."

"I do too," she said. Not just because she thought that's what she should say but it was the truth. And as Zac had pointed out when they'd signed their pact, if they stuck to the truth as they went along, it would be easier.

"Good," Juliette said. "I should be getting back but I'm not ready for everyone to be here. I hope that Adler is enjoying this quiet before the wedding events take over our lives."

"I'm sure she is. Last night she and Nick seemed to be taking a few moments to themselves. My mom said that she wished she'd done more of that."

"Your mom has always been so wise about relationships," Juliette said.

"You have too. I mean you and Mr. B are a really strong couple," Iris said. She'd heard the gossip about August Bisset's affair that had led to a reconciliation and the subsequent birth of Zac's youngest sibling and only sister, Mari. But since then it seemed that Juliette and August had been solid.

"Thank you for saying that. It hasn't been easy but we are stronger today because of it."

Iris couldn't help but sigh at the way she'd said that. "I want that someday."

"I hope you don't have the rocky road to it that I did," Juliette said.

"If I do, I hope I weather it as gracefully as you did," she said. "I don't feel like exercising. Care to join me for a mimosa before you head back home?"

"I'd love to. I think it's just what I need this morning. I keep thinking about Musette. She'd be completely trying to take over Adler's wedding and I know she'd love every minute of it," Juliette said, referring to Adler's deceased mom.

"It must be hard for you, but I know that Adler thinks of you as her second mom," Iris said.

"And she's my first daughter. I know that sounds bad but I had Adler before Mari and I've always thought of her as mine."

"You two have such a close relationship," Iris said. "I know it means a lot to Adler."

They walked back up toward the resort and went to the restaurant in the lobby for a light breakfast and mimosas. As they were finishing up, Iris's phone pinged. She glanced down to see it was a text from Zac.

Are you okay?

"Excuse me, I have to answer this," Iris said to Juliette.

"Go ahead. I'm going to finish this drink and then

head back to the big house. I'm glad we ran into each other this morning."

"Me too." Iris said goodbye, then typed out a response to Zac after Mrs. B left.

I'm in the lobby restaurant with your mom. I'll be back in the room in a few minutes.

My mom?!

Worried? ;)

No... Should I be?

No!

She settled the bill and sat there, taking her time with the final sip of her mimosa. Talking to the older woman this morning had relieved some of the tension she'd been carrying. It was clear that no matter how together a woman appeared on the outside, men and relationships could be a struggle. And in a weird way, that reassured her.

Waking up alone was nothing new to Zac, but when he rolled over and realized that Iris was gone, he wondered if he'd pushed too hard last night. He had a shower, thinking she must have gone for coffee. Then he shaved because he was going to be seeing his father for lunch. And there was no use going into that encounter with one hair out of place.

August Bisset could be charming, and there were a lot of times when Zac actually enjoyed being with his father. But not in social situations where he had to rule the room and the conversation. In such circumstances, his father wasn't afraid to point out the flaws in any of his children. It had been drilled into them to be the best from…well, for as long as Zac could remember.

After he'd shaven and gotten dressed for lunch, he started to worry about Iris. Where was she?

Was she okay?

He fished his cell phone out of his pocket and texted her. He wished he'd thought to tell her to turn on Find My Friends so he'd know exactly where she was, but he hadn't. He was stuck waiting for her to respond.

He saw the dancing dots on his screen and felt a sense of relief until she texted back that she was with his mom.

Dear God. That had *bad idea* written all over it. What were they talking about? He didn't even want to know.

She was cute and funny in her reply, which eased his mind about the night before. He'd be cool today. He was her hired date, and he'd give her what she'd paid for and a little bit more. If he focused on Iris, then he'd be able to deal with his dad without issue.

Or at least that was his hope.

He heard the door open and glanced over to see Iris entering the living area of their suite. She had on a pair of flower-print leggings and a tank top that hugged her curves. After the night they'd spent to-gether, he shouldn't want her again, but he did. She smiled at him and raised her eyebrows as she took in his navy pants, button-down oxford shirt and loafers.

"You're ready really early," she said.

"Usually we have a family meeting before events like this, so I'm anticipating a text from Carlton," he said.

"Good to know. Who's Carlton? Is that your dad's PR guy?" she asked.

"Yeah, he is. He kind of goes over the family image and the dos and don'ts for the event. Normally I'm not in town so I get to miss them, but I'm pretty sure I can't skip this one."

"Probably not. I'm going to shower and get dressed for the day. Should I plan to meet you later or come with you?"

He rubbed the back of his neck. "I'd like you to come with me. I mean, you don't have to, but if you are there, you're going to up my image rating."

She shook her head. "Your image rating is already pretty high."

"With you maybe," he said. "But I'm not as pol-ished as Dad and Carlton would like. And I seem okay now, but when you see me next to Dare, Logan and Leo, I do seem like the scruffy one."

"Good thing I like scruffy."

"Good thing," he said.

She gave him a little wave as she walked toward the bedroom. "I better get moving."

He leaned back against the sofa and turned on

ESPN as he waited for her. She'd been so peppy this morning. He'd thought she'd be dwelling on what had happened last night.

Well, hell.

She was ignoring it, wasn't she?

Was she going to pretend that nothing had happened?

Should he?

He knew that he couldn't do that. He wasn't built that way. But she was in full-on wedding-pact mode and that meant they were the picture-perfect couple. He had planned to use their arrangement to sooth his father and keep the criticism at bay, but now that he knew Iris was back to just playing a role, it bothered him. He wanted her to talk about last night or at least be thinking about it so that he'd know she was as affected as he was.

Didn't it mean anything to her?

He got up and went into the bedroom. He stood there, staring at the closed bathroom door until he heard the shower shut off. Then he ran for the bed and lay down on it, trying to look casual as the door opened and a cloud of steam preceded Iris into the room.

"What are you doing in here?"

"Waiting for you? We're lovers now, angel face," he said.

"I know but that was last night. The wedding stuff starts today. This is the contracted thing—"

"I'm not going to embarrass you but I'm also not going to pretend that last night and the other night didn't happen. There is more between us now than a contract."

She put her hand on her chest and toyed with her diamond necklace. "You know it still has to end, right?"

"Yes, of course, I'm not sticking around, hoping you'll put a ring on my finger," he said. "I have other commitments, as well."

"Good. Then I see no reason for you not to be in here."

But she didn't smile or talk to him while she got ready and he knew that something had changed between them again. They weren't closer now; there was a new barrier between them and he had the feeling it came from both of them ignoring the truth of what they felt and wanted to say.

Iris didn't want him as her lover while she was doing the wedding stuff this weekend. And he wanted her to be that. He wanted more from her than he'd contractually asked for and it was too late. He'd signed the agreement and he had to live up to it.

And he would. Come hell or August Bisset.

Iris didn't like the fact that Zac was on the bed, but she wasn't about to let him see he had shaken her. And he did have her in a state. Enough of one that she'd had to leave the room to clear her head and get it on straight. Which was when she'd run into his mom.

Ever since Thea had grabbed her phone and responded to Graham's text, nothing had been in her control. Her sister had goaded her without even realizing what she was doing. It wasn't Thea's fault that Iris always had to appear to be in control. And as much as she hated to admit it, it wasn't Zac's fault she'd blurred the lines between them.

She could admit that the first time she'd fallen into bed with him had been sheer lust. She hadn't had that kind of experience with a guy before. But she'd been hot for him. The second time… Hell, she had no excuse. Last night had been a slip in judgment and from where she stood in the slightly steamy bathroom, pretending she was still putting on her makeup, it seemed downright stupid.

He was hot and sweet and unexpected. And not for her. She wasn't trying to talk herself out of a good thing; she was reminding herself of her reality. She couldn't let the romance of Adler finding a great guy influence her. It didn't matter that she'd wanted a man to grow her brand into "coupledom." Zac wasn't that guy—he was only acting the part.

No amount of sex was going to change that.

But would it hurt her to keep having sex with him?

That was the million-dollar question.

She wanted to be a modern woman and say no. She could have sex with a guy and not fall in love with him. After all, look what had happened with Graham. But that had been bad sex. Not the melt-her-panties-off sex she had with Zac. That kind of sex made a girl dream of something more. Something forbidden and as hard to find as a unicorn in Times Square. And as much as she was all about her preppy, practical lifestyle, she was still a dreamer at heart. Underneath her Lilly Pulitzer navy dress with the white embroidery, she was dreaming of a man who'd stand by her side.

The knock on the door startled her and she put her hand to the diamond charm on the necklace before opening the door.

"You okay?" Zac asked.

He looked so sincere and sexy, dressed up to impress his parents. She wanted to tease him about it but frankly she got it. It didn't matter how grown-up or successful she became, she still wanted her parents' approval and it made her fall a little bit more for him that he wanted his.

"Yeah," she said. Her heart wasn't in putting up her normal shield this morning. Or at least not with him.

"We said no lies between us."

She sighed and brushed past him, trying not to let the scent of his aftershave send sensual tingles of awareness through her body, but she couldn't help remembering how strong that scent had been on his naked chest last night.

"I know," she said, going to the wardrobe where she'd stored her shoes and pulling out a pair of strappy white sandals that would give her a few extra inches of height. "But you're throwing me off my game, Zac."

"What? How am I doing that?" he asked.

She wished she could be Thea and just bluntly tell him that sex was making her addle-brained, but she wasn't her twin. She was Iris, and there was no way she was going to bring up sex now. They were on their way to lunch with his entire family, and she had to keep the new girlfriend act going.

"Nothing. I think I'm just tired this morning and nervous about meeting your family."

He nodded, then walked over to her and put his hand on her shoulder. "They're going to be so impressed that you're with me, you're not going to have to worry about anything. I'm the black sheep of the family."

Only the Bissets would consider an America's Cup team member the black sheep. She smiled and realized he'd done it again: eased her nerves by being himself. She had to find a way to make her feelings more casual. But everything about him made her want to cling.

She wasn't a clinger.

She didn't want to be the woman Graham had accused her of being.

Heck, was she reacting this way because she was trying to prove something to Graham?

She hoped not. She wouldn't be that petty and spiteful. But she always knew a part of her would love to rub in his face that she'd had a fabulous night of orgasms in Zac's arms.

She groaned.

"Iris?"

"Sorry. I just had the worst thought."

"Want to share it?"

"No, you'll think I'm a lunatic."

"Now I have to know what it was," he said, with that crooked smile of his.

"You know that guy who broke up with me, forcing me to hire you?" she asked. "Well he called me a cold fish because I couldn't climax with him and said lots of other mean things about me in the sack. And I was just thinking I wish I could tell him about last night. I think the issue was him, not me."

Zac smiled at her, pulled her into his arms and kissed her with passion. When he lifted his head, he said, "Angel face, it definitely wasn't you."

She put her arms around his shoulders and kissed him back, pouring all her fears and hopes into the embrace. When she stepped back, she told herself that was the last behind-closed-doors kiss they'd share. From now on, everything between them would be for show.

Really.

Thirteen

Juliette stood in the corner of the large conservatory that her mother always used for welcoming guests when the weather allowed. The July sky was gorgeous. Juliette almost wished she were the kind of woman to allow herself to believe in things like signs from heaven because she could have sworn that it was her sister looking down on them and giving Adler a perfect day.

But she didn't.

Her husband had changed his jacket three times, wanting to appear casual as he welcomed his one-time friend—and now enemy for more than thirty-five years—to lunch. Over the years Juliette had seen newspaper articles and some photos occasionally of Tad and his wife, Cora, but August always left events if they showed up so she'd never met them. Watching him try had always been the one thing that she hadn't been able to resist about him. August was a big man with big appetites, big ambition and a very big temper, but she'd glimpsed the vulnerability in him that he hid from the world.

They'd been married almost forty years so she knew that was to be expected.

"There you are, Jules," her mother said as she entered the room. "I have Michael and his staff ready with the welcoming drinks. I assume most of our guests will drink but he told me you asked him to include a nonalcoholic one, as well."

"I did, Mother. I hope you don't mind," she said. "I'm not sure what to expect from the Williams family, but I wanted to give everyone a choice."

"Good thinking."

Her mom had a way of making her feel like her party-hosting skills had stopped developing when she'd been throwing tea parties for her dolls even though she had a reputation for throwing the best parties in the Hamptons.

"Thanks."

"Do you really think she might make you a grandmother?" her mom asked.

"I don't know. And we shouldn't be discussing this now. Though I am ready," Juliette admitted.

"I am too. And what's with your boys? I thought they'd be more like Auggie and marry young, but they seem to be waiting," her mother said.

"They are like Auggie but on the business side,

not in terms of starting a family," Juliette said. All of her children were determined to make their mark on the world, and she didn't blame them. She'd often wondered if she'd had a career whether her marriage would have been different. Her life certainly would have. She might not even still be married to Auggie.

They heard the door open and Juliette was glad that the guests had started arriving. She liked socializing because it distracted her from her own thoughts and her own life.

"Gran," Zac said, coming into the conservatory with Iris Collins on his arm.

Iris was too sophisticated for her son, and if Juliette were being honest, she thought the younger woman was a little too prim. Zac liked his women more…well, sporty for one thing. And loose but not in a negative way.

"Zac, so good to see you. Your mother and I are both delighted you're back from Australia," her mom said as she went to hug him.

Juliette hugged Iris and then stepped back to hug Zac. Her boys were all taller than her now and his hug engulfed her. She held him longer than she knew she should, but she'd missed this tall blond boy of hers. He always made sailing seem like it was a gentleman's sport but she knew it was dangerous and she worried about him.

"Mom," he said, kissing her on the forehead.

"Sweetie," she answered. "Tell me why you were in Boston and how you met Iris. I know that's where it happened but the details are murky."

Zac put his arm out, drawing Iris in to the curve of his body. "Nothing murky about it, Mom. I quit my old America's Cup team and was in Boston looking for sponsors for my run in the next one. If I asked Dad, there'd be strings attached. Iris's father runs an investment group and we met when I was waiting to speak to him."

"I stumbled and he caught me," Iris said.

Zac looked down at Iris and winked and suddenly Juliette loved seeing her son with this woman. There was something about them that made her want to smile.

"Your dad won't be happy about the investment but I think everything else will be fine," Juliette said.

"I know but once I caught Iris I told myself not to let her go. It's not every day I meet a woman like Iris."

"So true," Nick Williams said, coming up behind Zac and clapping him on the shoulder.

Juliette smiled at Adler's fiancé. She'd met him a few times before and found him to be a very likeable man. But, of course, he was a thorn in Logan's side, always foiling his business deals and trying to beat him to market. So she understood that not everyone in her family was happy to see him, not to mention that he was marrying Adler.

"Hey, man," Zac said, turning to shake Nick's hand as Adler came in with an older woman.

There was something familiar about the tall brunette, Juliette thought as she came closer. Then their eyes met and both women froze. *Dear God.*

It was the other woman who'd been in labor the night Juliette had given birth to her unnamed still-born baby. Except she was a brunette now, not a blonde, and she wore the trappings of wealth as easily as if she'd been born to it.

Was this Cora Williams? The girl—Bonnie, she'd said her name was. Bonnie Smith. They'd both been in that post-delivery room crying. Juliette because she'd lost her baby that she'd hoped would save her marriage and Bonnie because she'd been cut off from her family, had no job and no way to support twins.

She remembered that moment when they'd realized there was a solution that would serve them both. If Juliette raised one of the fraternal twins as her own son, it would solve their problems.

Juliette had made a deal that only she, Bonnie and the nurse Jennifer had known about. They'd switched her stillborn child for one of the healthy boys. Juliette had given Bonnie a large sum of money from her private trust fund so she could go back to school and raise her son. Jennifer had taken a small sum to falsify the documents.

There wasn't a day that went by that she didn't think about the deal she'd made. How her Logan wasn't really hers. But until this moment she'd expected to keep the secret until her grave.

She'd never met Nick's parents…that meant that Nick was probably the other twin. She saw stars and thought she was going to pass out.

Crap.

This wasn't good.

The woman… Cora. Heck, she remembered everything about that night but at the time she'd called herself Bonnie Smith.

"Auntie Jules, this is Nick's mom, Cora," Adler said, bringing them both face-to-face. Cora seemed as shocked as Juliette felt.

But manners guided her and Juliette put out her hand. "So nice to meet you."

"You, as well," Cora said, but her hands were clammy. "I feel like I know you from all of Adler's stories."

"Me too," Juliette said. She knew they needed to talk but not now. Not today.

"Adler, is this your fiancé? I'm so eager to meet him and get to know his family," Auggie said as he came in.

Cora turned and Juliette saw the look on her husband's face as he saw her. She knew that look. Cora and Auggie had been lovers.

"Cora?"

"August," Cora said, then turned to Juliette. "You never said your husband was August Bisset."

"I didn't know you knew him."

"We need to talk," Cora said.

"I think we do," Juliette said.

Zac saw the color leave his mother's face and the shock on his dad's when he saw Nick's mom. Nick looked at him and they both seemed to be of the same mindset. Carlton had entered the room and looked at Cora and then blanched.

"Why is Bonnie Smith here?" Carlton asked as he came into the room. The older man had been his father's PR man and spin doctor since the beginning of his career. In fact, Zac had never been at a family meeting that wasn't chaired by Carlton. He was the one who cleaned up messes for the family. There were times when Zac liked the older man; he was nicer than his father. But there were other times when Carlton could be tough as nails. This was one of those times.

"Bonnie? This is my mother. Cora Williams," Nick said, stepping to Cora's side and putting his arm around her shoulders. "Is there a problem?"

"Don't worry about it, Nicky. I need to speak to August and Juliette alone. Will you keep an eye out for your dad?" Cora said.

Nick pulled his mom aside, away from everyone else, and Adler was looking at Zac's mom like she wanted to ask a million questions, but she wasn't saying a word. His father just walked out of the room with Carlton, turning around briefly. "Vivian, may we use your study?"

"Of course, Auggie."

"Ladies, will you please join me in there?" August asked.

Zac watched as his mom nodded but Nick stepped in front of Cora. "I don't think so. She's not going anywhere with you. I want to know what's going on. Why are they calling you Bonnie?"

"I agree with Nick," Adler said, going over to her fiancé and taking his hand. "What's going on?"

Juliette stood up and looked at Iris and Gran, and both of the women walked out of the room. But Zac stayed. This was his family and he wanted to know what was happening.

The butler closed the door to the conservatory. The groups in the room formed an odd triangle. Zac and his mom were on one side, his father and Carlton on another and Nick, his mom and Adler finished the formation. His father looked like he was going to lose his temper, his mom looked scared and Cora looked defensive.

He glanced over at Adler. She looked pale and afraid.

"Dad, how do you know Nick's mom?" Zac asked.

"I don't think you should be—"

"Just answer him, August. Tell our son how you know Nick's mom," his mom said.

From the tone of his mom's voice, Zac had the sinking feeling that Cora had been one of his father's other women. God, this was a mess. Had his father become her lover to get back at his rival Tad Williams?

"They were friends," Carlton said. "A long time ago. She was an intern who worked at the company just after Darien was born."

"Friends?" Nick asked, looking down at his mom. "With August Bisset?"

"Yes, dear," Cora said. "It was before I knew your father. We were friends."

"How do you know Juliette?" Nick asked. "Were you all friends?"

His mom's shoulders straightened and she shook her head. "No. That's not how we know each other. I met your mom the night I gave birth to Logan."

"We were in the hospital together. Both of us. In that rural hospital in the middle of a storm."

August looked at Cora and then shook his head. "You gave birth the same night as Jules?"

"I did," she said. "Unfortunately, I was a single mom and Juliette was kind to me."

"I know how hard it can be," Zac's mom said.

There was more to it. He could feel it in the room. A single woman giving birth at the same hospital as… Zac looked at his dad as he came to a conclusion that he hoped was wrong. Had his dad been Cora's lover? Was he Nick's father? *Hell.* He hoped not because then this entire wedding weekend was going to be a lot tougher than he'd thought it would be.

"Dad?"

"Zac."

"Is Nick your—"

"Niece's fiancé?" Carlton asked. "Because that's really the only question that makes sense, Zachary."

"Carlton, enough. It's just us. I want the truth," Zac said. "Adler deserves that. Hell, I think we all do."

He turned to look at Nick, who was staring down at his mother, and he saw the truth on the older brunette's face. She started to cry and before anyone could say anything else, the door burst open and Tad Williams walked in. He went straight to his wife's side. "What did that bastard say to you?"

But Cora couldn't answer. She just shook her head

and Tad pulled her into his arms. Nick was looking at his mother and then back at August and then he just walked out of the room. Adler ran after him and Zac wondered if he should leave, but when he started to go, his mom held on to his wrist, keeping him by her side. He looked over at her.

"Please."

He nodded and put his arm back around her shoulder. Zac knew he shouldn't be surprised because his father had never been a one-woman man. But in recent years he'd started to mellow and settle down. He'd been a good husband to his mom since Mari's birth. But this was a secret from the past and it was coming back to bite them. The kind of secret that could hurt them all. Not like the secret he and Iris had. That one was just between the two of them.

He'd made damned sure of that. "Dad, is Nick your son?"

"What?" Tad asked. "What is he talking about?"

Juliette had never felt like this before. She knew that Nick was August's child, which meant that Logan, the twin she'd raised, was August's child too. She'd always felt bad about deceiving her husband but now she felt sick. This complicated game that she and August had been playing with each other for forty years was now going to ensnare too many other people. And their sons would be hurt. Mari had been the product of their reconciliation after August's blatant affair in the early '90s but this was from almost a decade earlier. At the time, Juliette had never suspected her husband was having an affair.

She'd had some postpartum depression after Darien's birth and it had taken her a long time to get pregnant with her second child. The pregnancy had made things start to feel better between them. She had the feeling now that she'd been fooling herself. Because Cora had been pregnant at the same time with who she now truly believed were August's twins.

"I asked a question," Tad said.

"Tad, honey, August and I—"

"She worked for me, Tad. After you left the company, we had those interns come in and Bonnie—I mean Cora—was one of them."

Zac knew there was bad blood between Tad Williams and his father but not being a part of the day-to-day operation at Bisset Industries, he didn't know the details.

"Did he work for you?" Zac asked.

"I was an intern at the company for a short while until your father had me fired," Tad explained.

"You weren't performing up to expectations," August said.

"Whatever. How could you have an affair? You had a new wife and baby at home," Tad said.

"You're right, I did," his dad said. "I can make no excuses, only apologies. I wasn't the man I am today. When I saw something I wanted, I went after it. I didn't care who I hurt. And, Jules, my love, you know I regret that. I don't regret it if Nick is my son.

Cora was my lover at about that time. But I assumed he was your son."

"No, Cora and I started dating when Nick was three months old," Tad said. "Cora?"

"August is the father. I never told him I was pregnant. I ended things as soon as I realized that he had a wife and baby at home."

Zac wasn't sure what to say. This wasn't at all what he'd been expecting when he'd come to his gran's house for lunch with Adler's fiancé's family.

The conservatory doors opened again, and this time Logan and Leo walked in. Both of his brothers came straight toward him and his mom.

Logan put his hands on his hips, "What's going on? Adler is in tears. I really couldn't understand a word she said but she mentioned Dad…"

"Oh, God," Zac said. "Dude, there's no easy way to say this but it seems like your archenemy in business might be related to us."

"What the f—!" Logan didn't handle the news well. He turned on their father, who held his hands up.

"I just learned about it a second ago," their dad said.

Their mom put her hand to her throat and walked out of the conservatory and August followed.

"No one talks to the press. We need a meeting to figure out how to do this properly," Carlton said. "Mr. and Mrs. Williams, do you have a PR person, or would you like me to run point on this."

"We don't have a PR person," Cora said. "Nothing like this happens to us."

"I'll handle it for you," Carlton said, patting Cora on the arm. "Don't worry. This isn't going to be a big deal."

"I guess when you're used to cleaning up after August Bisset, it seems that way to you," Tad said. "But we are straight shooters. The Williams family doesn't cover up the truth."

Carlton nodded. "I know you and August have had issues in the past, but there is no way that you and your wife look good in this scenario if you go public with just the truth. August has a child he knew nothing about. You can see how that will play in the press."

Cora started crying and Tad put his arm around his wife. Zac walked over to them. He wasn't involved in the Bisset business. He felt that of all his brothers, he was the one who could liaise most easily with the Williams family.

"Carlton will make this right for all of us," Zac said. "He's not going to do anything that will put you in a bad light, Mrs. Williams. Isn't that right?"

"Of course. I'm sorry if it seemed I might," Carlton said. "We just have to cover all of the bases."

"I can't do this right now," Cora said.

"You don't have to," Carlton said. "I'm sorry I came on strong. Would you both come with me and we can figure out how you want to handle this announcement? I can tell you from past experience that we want to be the ones controlling the narrative."

Carlton led the Williamses out of the room and Zac turned back to his brothers. He hadn't seen them in person in over six months. "This isn't how I envisioned our reunion."

"Damn," Leo said, coming over to hug him. "It's good to see you, but what the hell happened?"

"Let's go get some cold ones and I'll tell you," Zac said.

"I can't," Logan said. "Is Nick really related to us? I mean, I hate that guy. I know Adler's marrying him and I was willing to be cordial but he can't be our half brother. I mean, he's the worst."

Zac clapped his older brother on the shoulder and squeezed. "I think he is. We'll figure out how to deal with him. Maybe he's not as bad as you imagine."

"Who's not?" Dare asked, coming into the room. He had his phone in one hand and a whiskey glass in the other. "Carlton told me you'd catch me up."

"We're all going to need something to drink," Leo said, leading them out of the conservatory to the lounge down the hall with the built-in bar. Iris and Gran were already sitting there and the women glanced up as they came in. Zac heard his brothers talking to his grandmother but he ignored them as Iris smiled at him. Who knew their charade would be the least exciting secret this weekend?

Fourteen

Iris didn't know how to help the actual situation they were in, but she did know how to be a good friend. When Adler came to the doorway and Iris saw the tears on her friend's face, she didn't even hesitate. She grabbed her friend's hand and took her upstairs to the bedroom that she knew Adler used when she was at her grandmother's house.

"What's going on?" she asked. "How's Nick?"

"Nick's mad. He's mad at his mom, his dad and August. It's just too much. You know I never thought that he'd have anything like this happen in his life. Oh, my God, this is something I'd expect from my dad. He's going to be completely crazy about this. He told me that I couldn't escape the chaos of life," Adler said.

Her friend was rambling and pacing around the bedroom. Iris saw that her hands were shaking.

"It's okay. Chaos is your friend," Iris said. "Your dad is going to be protective. Is he on Nantucket yet?"

"I don't know. I was supposed to text him when everyone was here. He was planning to come over and diffuse the tension between the Bissets and the Williamses," Adler said. "Given these new developments, I don't think even Dad can do that."

Adler stopped in front of the big bay window looking out at the ocean and Iris went over and hugged her. "What do you want me to do?"

"Make this all go away," Adler said.

"I can do that. We can leave Nantucket and go off grid until this passes."

Adler started crying and Iris hugged her friend harder. She didn't know how to fix this. She didn't know what impact Nick's paternity was going to have on Adler. Clearly she and Nick weren't related, as Nick was Cora and August's son; Adler wasn't a blood relation to August. But still, this was the kind of thing that Adler hated. She didn't like the jet-set party scene, or the bohemian live-for-the-moment mind-set. She wanted normal.

"Nick was supposed to be my Cory."

"I know," Iris said. Adler was referring to Cory from *Boy Meets World*. Growing up, the show had been their favorite to escape into. They'd loved that family dynamic and Adler had craved it for herself.

Adler's phone started ringing but she didn't make a move to see who it was.

"Want me to handle that?"

"Who is it?"

Iris glanced down at the screen. "It's your dad."

"Let me talk to him," Adler said. She took the phone and Iris stepped away to give her some semblance of privacy.

Iris was worried about Nick and Adler. This wasn't the news they needed two days before their wedding. She pulled out her own phone and texted Nick to ask if he was okay.

She got back a thumbs-up emoji.

She couldn't leave Adler and she knew that Nick needed someone. She didn't have any of his siblings' phone numbers and she wasn't sure if it was the right solution or not but she texted Zac.

Would you go and check on Nick? I think he's alone and he might need someone to listen.

She got an almost instant response. Where is he?

Iris used the location service on her messaging app. Nick was at the yacht club. Probably in the bar. At least he wasn't driving.

She sent the information to Zac.

On my way to see him. I'll tell him you sent me. He might not want to talk to me.

At least he won't be alone. Thanks.

No problem. This wasn't how I saw the day going.

Me either.

I'm glad you're here with me.

Me too.

She didn't have to think too hard about it. Seeing the people she loved, a family she thought she knew, thrown into a maelstrom was hard to witness. Knowing that they were going to have to put on a good public face when all of the guests started arriving made her glad she was here. She could help with that. And being with Zac was giving her a safe base to do it from. She wasn't just Adler's friend; she was posing as Zac's girlfriend and this family drama included her.

Adler collapsed back on the bed as she ended her call with her dad. "What am I going to do?"

Iris went over and lay down next to her on the bed. "About what?"

"Nick. The wedding. Everything. This isn't what I signed up for."

"Do you love him?"

"I thought I did."

"Do you still want to marry him?"

Adler leaned up on her elbow. "I don't want the media circus that this could become but I do want to marry him. But Nick isn't the same guy now."

"I wish it were simple. I've never seen two people as in love as you guys were," Iris said. "Are you strong enough to handle this?"

"I don't know," Adler said. "Our love has been easy. We've never been tested like this."

"You've handled way worse," Iris said.

"But that was easy because I was sort of removed when dad was having his issues with the media," Adler said. "It's simpler when I'm not in the direct spotlight."

"I know. But you won't be for long. If I know your dad, he'll do something outrageous to keep the attention off you. He loves you more than any other person on the planet."

Adler nodded. "That wouldn't be good either because he's just started to settle down. He can't go back to being outrageous again and living that rock'n'roll lifestyle. I mean he's barely recovered—"

"He won't," Iris interrupted. It was hard enough for Adler to worry about Nick, let alone having to worry about her dad.

"Oh, my God. I shouldn't have let Nick leave alone. I freaked out about my perfect wedding," Adler said. "He's just found out a man he hates is his father."

"I know. I sent Zac to find him," Iris said.

"I think I need to go to him. We have to talk about what this means for us."

Iris agreed. Her friend was too emotional to drive so she went with her. They snuck out of the house because Adler didn't want to risk running into any of her cousins or her uncle on the way.

* * *

Zac picked up two Maker's Marks, straight, before approaching Nick. The other man looked like Zac had felt when he'd walked away from the UK team he'd been part of and decided to strike out on his own. He'd had no idea if any of his friends would come with him and it had been a lonely, lonely feeling.

"Nick, would you like some company?"

Nick glanced up at him and for the first time since Zac had known him—which, granted, wasn't long— the man didn't look at ease. His eyes were bloodshot and Zac noticed that his knuckles were scraped as if he'd punched a wall.

"I brought a double, figured you could use it," Zac said.

Nick took the drink and pushed the chair opposite him out with his foot. Zac sat down and took a swallow once Nick drank some of his.

"Iris sent me. I would have come on my own but had no way of getting in touch with you."

"Thanks, man. I'm not sure what the hell is going on and I know I'm not the best company right now."

"That's cool. I spend most of my time on the ocean fighting against the wind and waves and trying to prove I'm nothing like the rest of my family," Zac said.

"Your family…"

"It's yours too, right? I mean we don't have to talk about it but I want you to know that we're not as bad as you might think."

Nick downed the rest of his whiskey. "I can't do this right now. I was already a little nervous thinking of marrying Adler and starting my own family and then to learn that everything I knew about myself was a lie…"

"It wasn't a lie," Zac said. "I don't know much about your family but your dad is Tad Williams. No matter what biological matter my dad contributed, Tad raised you and the man I saw today is a good man. He defended your mother and mine."

"He is a good man. I've always wanted to be just like him," Nick said.

Zac realized that Nick might not know it but he had a better relationship with Tad Williams than he ever would have had with August Bisset. August was mellowing but he was still a difficult man to have as a father.

"That's good," Zac said. "Nothing's changed. Did you know he wasn't your biological father?"

"I did."

"Did your mom ever say anything about my dad?" Zac asked.

"She said she'd fallen for a man who was charming and funny, and when she'd realized he belonged to someone else, she left. She said he wasn't in the picture and that Tad was the only father I'd know."

Zac wished that had been the case. "I'm sorry."

"Thanks," Nick said, pushing the glass back and forth between his hands.

"Want another?"

"Yes. But I have to fix things with Adler. She tried to say things would be okay and I yelled at her."

"I think I'd do the same thing in your situation," Zac said. "That kind of news is hard to hear."

"It is, but Adler didn't deserve that. She was freaking out too, I know it, even though she didn't say anything."

"But she loves you," Zac said. "I've never seen her this happy before."

"That's the worst part about finding this out now. It's going to be a cloud over the wedding. Hell, I don't even know if she'll still marry me after I yelled at her the way I did."

The door to the bar opened. Zac caught sight of Iris and Adler. Leave it to Iris to get the couple back together and salvage the weekend. That was one of the things he admired about her. She didn't hesitate to do whatever she needed to in order to make things run smoothly.

Look at how she'd contracted him to be her man when she'd been dumped.

Where had that thought come from?

There was a hint of resentment inside him as he realized he might be just another quick fix that she was so good at administering.

"There's only one way to find out," Zac said to Nick. "Adler just walked in."

Nick pushed his glass to one side and sat up straighter. His shoulders went back and all the doubt and anger that had been dominating his expression and posture were subdued. It was as if he were putting on a show for Adler.

Instead, he was the confident man that Zac had seen the night before at dinner. He ran his hands over his hair and then noticed the scraped knuckles. Zac pulled his pocket square out and handed it to the other man. "Use this."

"Thanks."

Nick cleaned his knuckles, passing the square of fabric back just as the ladies arrived at their table.

Nick and Zac stood and when Nick turned to Adler, Zac looked away. They were hugging each other, and it was so intimate that really no one should be watching them.

He glanced at Iris and saw the longing on her face. She wanted what Adler and Nick had but she'd settled for a contracted boyfriend.

He wondered why. Was it convenience? Or was there something deeper that kept her from really committing to a man?

"Let's give them some privacy," he said.

She nodded and slipped her hand into his as they turned away. He looked down at their joined hands. After the morning they'd had, filled with lies and betrayals and secrets that should have stayed that way, he wondered what he was going to do about his woman he'd agreed to pretend to care for, since he had already realized that he had never been pretending with her.

She had gotten to him from the first moment they'd met and he should have done the smart thing and walked away. But she had him ensnared, and he had to admit he didn't mind it as long as she felt something for him.

Which he couldn't be sure of.

Iris walked with Zac to the other side of the yacht club bar, which wasn't very busy at this hour. She was worried about Zac. She knew he and his father had a contentious relationship and finding out that his dad had cheated on his mom…that had to be a blow.

"Are you okay?"

He held out a chair for her and nodded. "Do you want a drink?"

"I'm okay, but you can get one if you want to."

"I don't like to drink alone," he said.

"I'll have a Perrier with a lime," Iris said, realizing he needed something to do. She would bet that everyone in his family was doing their best to keep busy and not think about what had happened.

He walked to the bar and Iris realized she should probably cancel all of the filming she'd planned to do around the events for the day. She sent a text to her staff, letting them know that the family had decided to have a quiet day together and told them to enjoy the bonus day off. She also texted her friend Quinn, who was producing the televised wedding ceremony, and told her that Adler wasn't going to be available today.

Quinn called back instead of texting. Considering that Iris, Quinn and Adler had been good friends since their freshman year of college when they'd met at the sorority house, she wasn't surprised.

"Is Adler okay?"

"Yes. There was some unexpected drama with the Bissets and the Williamses and I don't know that she's in the right state to film. Just wanted to give you a heads-up."

"Thanks for that. Is she okay? I'm going to text her. Just send her some virtual hugs. I'm on the damn ferry right now. This thing seems to go slower and slower every time I get on it."

Quinn was a big city gal used to moving at a fast pace. Iris had once seen her friend pay for and bag up another woman's groceries because she was moving too slow. "There's nothing you could do if you were here sooner."

"Except see Ad and if needed, kick some Bisset butt. They have to be the trouble, right?"

"It's complicated," Iris said. "Text me when you get here. Do you need a ride?"

"No. The traffic will be heavy when the ferry gets in. I'm going to run to the hotel. I need to burn off some energy."

"Okay, I'll see you later then."

"Bye."

Zac set the glasses on the table before sitting down across from her. He rubbed the back of his neck and turned to look out at the ocean. His clean jaw and sharp blade of a nose gave him a gorgeous profile but then everything about him struck the right note for her.

"Wish you were out there?"

He turned back and took a sip of what looked like whiskey. "Yes and no. I mean, my mom would've been alone when she heard the news about my dad today if I hadn't been there."

"That was a shock," Iris said. "I was glad I got to escape."

"I bet."

He didn't say anything, just swallowed his whiskey in one long sip.

"Do you want to talk about it?"

"Which part?"

"Whichever part you want to," she said.

"I'm not sure. This isn't part of the contract."

"So? You said it yourself. We're friends, aren't we?" she asked. She had stopped thinking about the contract when shit had gotten real in the conservatory. It had made her feel very shallow to realize she'd been worried about showing up stag when something like this was going down.

"Are we?"

She wasn't sure if he was being cagey because of what he'd learned about his dad or if he had some beef with her. She knew if it were her, she'd want to fight with someone…probably Thea because she knew that she could say mean things to her sister and, in the end, Thea would forgive her.

"Yes, we are. Listen, I can't begin to imagine what you're feeling but if you need to talk or yell or go sailing or—"

"Have sex?"

Her eyes widened but she nodded. Whatever he needed. She hated to see the people she loved hurt… Wait, did she love him? She wasn't sure if she did because she'd never been in love before, but this felt… well, not like anything she'd experienced before.

"Yes. Even that. Whatever you need. I'm here," she said.

He reached for her hand and laced their fingers together. "I don't know what I need. I guess I'm in shock. I've always known my dad wasn't faithful to my mom. He had a very public affair before Mari was born. But I thought we knew the worst of him. Catting around on Mom while she was pregnant with Logan…that is something I can't forgive."

"You don't have to," Iris said. "You get to decide what you feel about that and if you can't get past it, then that's fine. He's always going to be your father, but you don't have to let him be a part of your life."

Zac nodded. "I know what you are saying but here's the kicker. I want him in my life. I've always worked so hard to make him proud. To prove that I was better than he was. And now, knowing in my heart how petty I want to be about this, I don't think I am any better."

Iris went around to sit next to him at the table. She put her arm around him and her chin on his shoulder. "No one is. That's something I had to figure out the hard way. But no one is better than anybody else. We are all messed up and trying to figure out how to get through each day. Your dad had a shock, as well. He screwed up and probably thought that he had put all of that in the past. And then today his mistakes were front and center for his entire family to see."

"You're right. I know you are," Zac said. He pulled her around onto his lap and just held her in his arms. She knew she should get up, that people would see them, but she didn't want to. She wanted to give as much comfort to this man she loved as she could. And it didn't matter what kind of image they presented to the world.

Nick took Adler to the new home he'd had built for them on Nantucket. She watched him pacing around the living room, that she'd had designed for their future. But as she looked around she saw it was all the things she wanted them to be and maybe not who they really were.

"What are we going to do?" she asked him.

"Do about what—the wedding?"

"Yes." What did he think she was talking about?

"I really don't know. We have all these people coming to Nantucket. If we cancel—"

"Are you thinking about not marrying me?" For the first time she had to face her fears about Nick. He was questioning everything about himself and his life. Maybe he was questioning a future with her, too?

"I don't know," he said, shoving his hands through his hair. "My gut says this isn't going to blow over easily. I want to manage it."

"I get that. Managing the news about your parentage should be the top priority. But are we going to do it as a team?"

He turned on her and she saw anger in his eyes. "Can we have one minute where it's not all about you, Adler? Is that possible?"

She took a deep breath and nodded. She was about to start crying and blinked rapidly to keep the tears from falling. "Take as much time as you need. I'm going to my gran's."

"Run away. That's what you do when life gets too real, isn't it?"

"It's what I do when I'm confronted with a bully who is lashing out because he doesn't want to admit he's hurting," she said. Her voice was low and rough from trying to choke back tears. "Let's have the clambake tonight and tomorrow we can figure out if we should still get married. We have a lot of people coming. Try to remember it's not all about you, either."

Adler left the room, tears streaming down her face. She wished her mom were here so she could talk with her about this. She had no idea how to handle Nick right now.

Was the man she loved gone? Had Nick disappeared when he learned he was August Bisset's biological son?

Fifteen

Iris and Zac ended up taking a lead role in entertaining the guests who were attending the clambake on Thursday evening. The elder Williams and Bisset couples had spent the day with Carlton coming up with the spin on today's revelations in case the story somehow got out to the press.

Iris just stayed by Adler's side and did whatever her friend asked her to do. It was odd to see Adler so fragile because she'd never been like that before. This thing with Nick had rattled her.

It was safe to say the couple hadn't resolved things. They were still going through with planned events but Iris could tell nothing was right.

Nick was drinking a lot; Iris had known him in his frat boy days so that was saying something. Zac was keeping pace with him and she had to say she was both surprised and happy to see that he was a really funny drunk. His brother Logan, who had the fiercest rivalry with Nick in business, had surrounded himself with a group of women that Iris wasn't sure were part of the wedding party. Leo, Zac's younger brother, was keeping an eye on Zac and Nick and running drinks back and forth to them. Nick's brothers, Asher and Noah, were hanging with Leo and Nick's sister Olivia was at Iris's side, helping Adler out.

The food had been prepared by a catering company Adler had hired, which meant there was little for them to do but keep the conversation going and that horrible truth buried.

Iris saw Toby Osborn before Adler did. He still had a full head of hair despite being sixty. He had a mustache and short beard and carried his legendary guitar, Martha Mae. He had his usual entourage with him, including his live-in girlfriend, whom Iris had met before and liked.

As soon as Adler saw her dad, she ran to him and he pushed his guitar around to his back and caught her. Iris knew that Adler had always wished for a more normal upbringing but there was no denying she had been well loved by her father. She was his world.

"What'd I miss?" Quinn asked, coming up beside her and handing her a gin and tonic.

"Nothing. The elders are back at the house having a meeting, Nick's getting drunk and Zac is helping him, and Toby's just arrived."

"Are you dating Zac?"

"That's what you got out of my rundown?" Iris asked.

"Well, I did see it on my newsfeed. He's not your usual type, is he?"

"Uh, no. Graham kind of put me off my usual type."

"Graham was a douche bag," Quinn said.

"Did everyone hate him?" Iris asked.

"Yes," Quinn said. "I'm glad you aren't with him anymore."

She glanced over at Nick and Zac, who were singing along to Sister Hazel's "All For You." She especially loved when they tried to harmonize and neither of them sang a note that was near the other's. Toby set Adler down and went over to the two would-be singers and joined in.

"Oh, my God, they're hilarious," Iris said, grabbing her phone so she could capture the moment. She knew that Nick would want to see this happy moment later, after a day that had been filled with so many ups and downs.

Zac caught her filming and wriggled his eyebrows at her. The next time the chorus came on, he gestured to her as if to say he only wanted to be with her. She knew he was drunk and kidding around but she wanted this to be true.

Adler came up beside her and looped her arm through hers and Quinn took her other arm. After the crazy day they'd had, she was so grateful to have these two women by her side. She wasn't sure that anything was going to come of her and Zac but she'd have this memory to last forever.

And after the way she'd seen the past come back to haunt August and Cora, she wondered if she shouldn't come clean about hiring Zac to be her man for the weekend. She didn't want that to come out at some odd time when they were both older and more established…maybe with other partners.

The thought hurt and dimmed her joy of the moment, but she had to be honest with herself. She loved Zac but that hadn't made her blind to how impossible it was for the two of them.

He was in the spotlight, dancing and singing and loving the attention, and she would never be comfortable out there. She needed her glam squad and her prepared scripts to be comfortable in front of the camera.

She stopped filming the video as the song ended. Toby started singing some of his hits and Adler drifted over to Nick and they walked down the beach. Quinn's phone went off and she turned away to take the call. Iris was left standing by herself. Zac was surrounded by his brothers. She watched him and realized that he always knew how to handle every situation and she envied that.

It was something she'd never been able to find in herself. She could only function with rules. She took a step backward as she realized that she had let herself love Zac because it was safe. She'd let her guard down, thinking her contract and her end date would keep her from getting hurt. Never realizing that letting her guard down was the thing she should have been avoiding.

It wasn't a certain type of man who could hurt her—it was herself. Her own flaws and fears had been driving her to this moment ever since she'd become an adult.

She looked at Adler, trying so hard to find a man who was nothing like her father and then finding out on the eve of her wedding that he had a scandalous secret, even though it was no fault of his own. Then Iris thought of her own secret with Zac, one she was 100 percent responsible for.

There was no way to protect herself from herself. She wished she'd realized this in Boston before she'd walked into that bar and seen that sexy man for the first time. She wished she'd had the strength to know herself and be real about her fear of being alone then. She wished… Hell, it hurt her to her core but she wished she'd never talked to Zac Bisset.

Without saying a word to anyone, she quietly left the party and went back to the hotel.

She was in her bed for a good four hours before she heard Zac in the other room with some other guys. They were laughing and shushing each other and she lay there alone in her bed, realizing that even paying for a man hadn't changed her.

Zac woke up with a fuzzy mouth on the couch of the suite he'd been sharing with Iris. He had one shoe on and his belt was removed but otherwise he was fully clothed. He blinked, surprised he didn't have a headache. But he'd been very well hydrated the night before. He blinked again, seeing the light through the window, and then Iris sitting in a chair opposite him. She watched him with that prim expression she had when she was in an awkward situation.

He scrubbed his hand over his face, felt the stubble on his jaw and something that might be a bruise later—did he punch Logan last night? Then he forced himself to sit up and tried to smile but the light was really bright and he had to close his eyes for a second.

"If you can manage it, I've put in an order for a bacon, egg and cheese biscuit for you," Iris said.

"You really are an angel. Coffee too?" he asked.

"Coffee too."

He knew he should go and wash up. He'd been in this situation before. Women didn't always respond positively when he came home drunk and passed out on the couch.

He washed his face, brushed his teeth and debated a quick shower. After a whiff of his clothes as he took them off, he decided that there was no debate and spent three minutes under the hot jets of water.

He felt closer to human as he left the bedroom dressed in a pair of basketball shorts and an old America's Cup team T-shirt. His food was on the table under a cloche, along with a cup of coffee and a plate of fresh fruit.

Iris sat at the table, looking so elegant and put together, like a woman with a mission on her mind.

"I'm sorry about last night. I knew Nick needed to

drink because I would in his situation. My brothers were being uptight and his were too, so someone had to be the one to break the ice," Zac said.

"That's okay. Honestly, you were so funny and probably exactly what everyone needed," she said.

He opened the cloche and took a bite of the bacon, egg and cheese biscuit, and closed his eyes. It was perfect. Exactly what he needed.

"What about you? I know I wasn't delivering on my duties last night," Zac said.

"About that," Iris said. "I think we can agree that your behavior last night can't be repeated. Starting today, I need you to be everything I asked for in the contract."

"I'll try," he said, taking another bite of the biscuit. Honestly, at this moment, he was only half listening to her. The food was making him feel a lot better.

"You'll do more than try or you will be in breach of our agreement and I will call my father and tell him that I don't think you're a good investment," she said.

That he heard.

He put his biscuit down and his hands on the table next to his plate. "Are you threatening me?"

"I am. I know your family is going through some messy things, but your first priority is the commitment you made to me."

"Other than last night, have I shirked my duties?"

"Last night was the first time you were supposed to be doing your duties in front of other people."

"I sang to you, Iris. Even Toby said that was romantic," Zac said.

"I came home about four hours before you did," Iris pointed out. "You didn't even notice I was gone... Not very romantic."

"Sorry I wasn't paying one hundred percent attention to you," he said. "I already apologized for last night."

"You did and I appreciate it. I'm just saying don't let it happen again."

She stood up and walked past him to go to the bedroom but he stopped her by catching her wrist lightly in his hand. "Are you okay?"

She nodded, tugged her hand free and kept on going.

But he knew she wasn't. He wanted to blame it on his hangover but he knew he was missing something. He'd done something last night that had changed the way that Iris was looking at him. Damn him if he could remember all of the details clearly enough to figure it out.

He finished his biscuit and coffee. He wanted to make this right. He stood up and went to the bedroom door, knocking on it before entering. She was standing in front of her wardrobe when he entered.

"Hey, I'm sorry about last night. Whatever you need today, I'll be there for you. I think we have the scramble golf tournament and you wanted me to pose for some photos, right?"

"Yes. My glam squad will be bringing some clothes for you and I'll text you when I need you.

I kind of like the stubble so if you want to leave it for this morning and then shave before tonight's rehearsal dinner—if it's still even on—that would be fine. Did you see Adler last night?"

"I don't remember," he said. "Angel face, I really am sorry. I never meant to drink like that. It's not every day I find out I have another brother."

She nodded. "I know. I'd be a monster not to understand it, and I definitely am not upset that you drank last night."

"Then what are you mad at me about?" he asked. "Don't deny it, you are upset with me."

She shook her head. "I'm upset with myself because I thought you were something that you aren't."

Something he wasn't. He'd been more himself with her than he'd ever been with anyone else and she still thought he was phoning it in.

He was tired, he knew that, and a wiser man than he would have kept his mouth shut. But hell, no one had ever labeled him the smart Bisset.

"I'm not what you thought?" he asked, approaching her as she turned away from the wardrobe to face him. "Iris, you hired a guy you met in a bar to be your boyfriend for a four-day wedding. What exactly were you expecting?"

"Don't get defensive, I wasn't attacking you," she said, folding her hands neatly in front of her.

And that right there was enough to push him over the edge. He'd seen glimpses of the real woman beneath all the prim and proper behavior but more times than not, this was what he was faced with.

Some cardboard cutout of the real woman. No man wanted that. Actually he felt safe in saying that no one wanted to have a relationship with someone who was always hiding behind the perfect smile, clothing and manners.

"I've gone above and beyond for you. I actually like you as a person most of the time, but I can't with this," he said, gesturing to her holding her coffee cup with one hand while smiling serenely at him. "It's not real. I get that we have a contract, but I've never been anyone other than myself with you. Who does that?"

"I do, according to you."

"You can't fight properly. Tell me what's on your mind. Don't worry about hurting my feelings or how it might make you seem human instead of a social media goddess with the great life. Just be you, Iris. Do you even know who you are?"

"Screw you, Zac. That's not a very nice thing to say. Of course, I know who I am," she said.

"That's it. Get mad, girl. Show me what's really bothering you," he said. He wasn't sure where this was going but after last night, learning that most of his life he'd been lied to by his father, he was tired of half-truths. He was no longer interested in playing a part. Any part. He was going to live life on his terms and he wasn't holding back. Iris should do the same.

"What's bothering me?" she said. "I don't think you really care that much, Zac. We both know you're only here until my dad and Collins Combined come through with your funding. Then you are off to train and race for three years. We both know that you are playing a role even though you want to pretend that you're, what, better than me, more honest than me? You're not. You're here dressing in jackets with pocket squares, shaving and trying to fit into a role as much as I am. You're judging me while excusing yourself."

"I didn't say I was disappointed in you," he pointed out.

"Well you didn't have to. I'm disappointed in myself. You know what's the matter this morning? My dad sent over some paperwork for both of us. He has assembled your investors and you will have the money wired into your account on Monday. And I know you'll be out the door. Sure, you'll be sweet and polite about it, but that's it. You'll move on.

"And while I watched you singing and dancing in front of the fire last night, I realized I didn't want you to leave. I didn't want to see you walk out of my life because I'm an effing idiot and fell in love with you. Sure, I knew I shouldn't. Hell, you're not even the kind of man I usually fall for. But you know that perfect image you're so sure I'm hiding behind—well, I wasn't. I was myself. Sorry I'm not more exciting and can't deliver nonstop fun the way you can, but that was me. Guard down and being totally myself."

He was stunned. He was pretty sure in the middle of her rant she'd said she loved him. Iris Collins, the most sophisticated, sexy, sweet, charming, smart woman he'd ever met, loved him. He'd lashed out because he knew he wasn't worthy. Even now he realized he'd let her down. Again.

He should apologize. He knew that. But his brain was working slowly this morning and Iris just shook her head and blinked a lot before she walked out of the hotel suite.

Why was she leaving?

He hadn't had a chance to tell her any of the things he needed to. He ran out after her, but she'd gotten in the elevator and was gone. His gut told him if he let her go, he'd regret this for the rest of his life.

This wasn't a moment where time was going to make things better. She needed him now.

He went to the balcony. They were only on the third floor and he climbed over and lowered himself onto the balcony below and then one more time until he was on the ground floor.

The gravel path was rough on his bare feet, but he made it around to the front of the building just as Iris exited. She had her large black sunglasses on and a sheath dress. He stood there with dirt and rock embedded in the bottom of his feet, looking like a beach bum instead of a Bisset.

He was never going to be the picture-perfect man on her arm, but he knew that no one would love her better or give her more adventure in her life.

Now to somehow show her that.

Sixteen

Iris walked straight past him and he realized that maybe it was better if he just let her go. She was definitely not thinking straight. He knew women tended to get all those romantic feelings during a wedding weekend and Adler and Iris were best friends.

He stood there next to the valet, barefoot and looking like he'd just come off a night of binge drinking, which he had. Watching the woman he loved more than he'd ever thought he could walk away from him was sobering. This was the reality of life with the two of them. They were both busy people and weekends like this would be the best they could hope for.

She deserved more, and in her own words, wanted more. Shouldn't he just let her have it? He watched her get into her sensible car and drive off and then he slowly made his way back into the hotel.

His brother Logan was slinking in, as well. He had his eyes shielded behind his Ray-Ban Wayfarers and as he saw Zac, he lifted his hand in a weak wave. His brother looked worse than Zac felt, and he wasn't sure how that was possible given that Zac's world was crumbling. Everything he'd ever believed about himself was shattered. He wasn't the man who was looking for another horizon—he had been looking for Iris. No other woman had ever made him feel like he was okay just as he was.

"Dude, you look rough," Zac said. "Where'd you go last night?"

"Took a trip down memory lane and I'm not sure how but we ended up in bed," Logan said. "I think it's going to end up biting me in the ass."

"Her too," Zac said. Logan hadn't always been the type-A, driven COO he was today. Once upon a time he'd been a very competitive kid with a girlfriend who liked to one-up him. Quinn had gone on to take television by storm. She was one of the top producers today. But Logan had caught up and maybe even moved past her, making a name for himself at Bisset Industries. It was interesting to think of the two of them hooking up. And it was just the distraction he needed after Iris walked away looking broken.

"Yeah, I know," Logan said. "What are you doing in the lobby looking like a hobo? If you have even the slightest chance of keeping a woman like Iris Collins, you have to up your game," Logan said. "Come up to my room and I'll get you some decent clothes."

"Thanks, bro," he said, trying to play it cool but knowing he failed when Logan put his hand on his shoulder. Everyone could see that he and Iris weren't meant to be. He should just take the investor money and start focusing on the one area where he was good. Sailing. Captaining a racing team. He could do that.

"You okay?"

"No. I screwed up, Logan. I have no idea how to fix it or if I should even try. I'm hungover. I might still be a little drunk. I've had the kind of morning that Dad should be having but he probably is too coldhearted to realize that everything is slipping out of his grip."

"Z, Dad's not the heartless monster that the media and Carlton play him up to be, you know that. Despite everything else happening right now. What's wrong that you are lashing out?"

He shook his head. He had no idea where to start. "Never mind."

"I'm on your side. I'm always on your side, no matter what happens. Talk to me. If there's one thing I'm good at, it's solving problems," Logan said.

He was good at it. "All right. I agreed to be Iris's plus one this weekend in exchange for her getting some investors for my America's Cup run. We both said it would be temporary, but it didn't feel that way until this morning. Now I don't want to let her go, but even you pointed out that she's too good for me and you hardly ever notice stuff like that."

Logan put his hand on Zac's arm and urged him to move out of the lobby. For the first time, Zac was aware of their surroundings—the fact that it was a crowded lobby and that people had been staring at the two of them.

Damn.

Hell.

He was the biggest asshole on the planet. He'd had blinders on because he wasn't used to anyone caring what he did when he was on land.

"Do you think they heard?"

"I have no idea, but let's get up to my room and figure out what's next," Logan said.

"She'll be ruined by this, Logan. I can't believe I didn't think before I spoke. She's all about image. I mean that's why we—"

Logan put his hand over Zac's mouth as they got on the elevator. The door closed and Logan dropped his hand. "Paparazzi are all here trying to get the scoop on the latest Bisset scandal. You have to stop talking."

"I know."

Zac didn't say another word until they were down the hall and in his brother's room. "Why aren't you staying at Gran's?"

"I didn't want to make Adler uncomfortable. I've been a douche about Nick and he's her groom. But I do love our cousin. I figured the least I could do was stay out of her way."

"Yeah, that's a good call. Nick's not a bad guy."

"I know. It's just that for as long as I can remember, I've always been trying to beat him. Sometimes

I do and other times I don't. I hate losing and he's a Williams, so it makes it harder to let it go," Logan said, tossing his sunglasses on the bed and then looking over at him. "Now about Iris... We need to get ahead of this before it comes out."

"What am I going to do?" Zac asked his brother. "I love her. I was trying to ask you how to win her back, but it seems impossible now, doesn't it?"

"Nothing is impossible. You told me that when we were teenagers. If you were smart enough to realize that back then, you can fix this," Logan said.

Zac wasn't sure his "wisdom" as a teenager was anything more than bravado, and he didn't know how to fix this. But he regretted that he might hurt her and had to try to make things right.

Iris didn't have a destination in mind as she left the hotel behind. She could think of only one person who actually needed her this morning and that was Alder. Sure Iris wanted to escape. She'd never been in love with anyone before and confessing it to Zac and having him just sort of blink at her wasn't the reaction she'd been hoping for. She'd had two break-ups fairly close together and honestly she had to say this one was affecting her way worse than the first.

Not that she and Zac had broken up. She started crying as she realized how messed up this truly was. She pulled her car off the road and just sat there for a few minutes, realizing that the only place she wanted to be was off Nantucket. But she couldn't do that to Adler.

She was trapped by her own bad decisions. She almost texted Thea something mean but it wasn't her sister's fault that she'd decided to choose a man to be her fab, fun plus one and Zac Bisset turned out to be the one. She couldn't have predicted it and she couldn't blame it on Thea.

She drove her car back to a public parking lot and left it there, walking toward the beach because going back to the room she was sharing with Zac was completely out of the question. She took her shoes off as soon as she was on the sand. Tendrils of hair started to escape from the chignon she'd put it up in, when she was still trying to pretend that she had it all together. She reached up and took the pins out, knowing that she was done fooling herself.

Since she'd gotten the internship with Leta Veerland, she'd promised herself she wouldn't waste a moment. That she'd craft a life that was successful and leave no room for failure and she'd done that. On every front except on the personal one. But there was no way she was ever going to be successful in a relationship unless she let herself be. The problem with men, and Zac in particular, was that she didn't want to be vulnerable to him. She didn't want him to see that she wasn't that social media person. The one with the fabulous life who made good choices. But until him, she'd never found a way to be comfortable with herself.

Now she had no choice and she was failing.

Big time.

She took a deep breath and tipped her head back,

letting the sea air sooth that troubled part of her soul. She'd taken a risk, a real gamble, when she'd approached Zac. And it had given her so much more than she'd expected. She had to let herself have that.

Her phone vibrated but she ignored it. She wasn't going to respond to anything right now. She needed this walk on the beach to gather her thoughts and regain her equilibrium. She knew she was the maid of honor at the wedding and Adler might need her.

Adler. Something had been up with her and Nick last night. Iris pulled out her phone to text Adler and saw on the Find My Friends app that she was on the beach as well. She walked toward her position and found her friend standing on the shore just staring out at the water.

"Hey, Ad," she said, coming up behind her and hugging her. "Everything okay this morning?"

Adler wiped her eyes and immediately Iris knew it wasn't.

"Nick and I had a big fight last night. I'm just not sure if we should cancel everything. He was too hungover this morning to discuss it and said whatever I decided he'd go along with."

That didn't sound like the Nick she knew. "He didn't mean that."

"I'm not so sure. He's reeling from learning that August is his father."

Iris held Adler's hand. "I know, but he loves you."

"He did."

"Stop that. This is just bridal jitters on steroids. He's not himself because of the news, but I'm sure how he feels about you hasn't changed. Do you want to cancel the wedding?"

Adler hesitated and Iris's heart, already sore and aching, broke for her friend. Men. Love was kicking her ass and now Adler's ass, too.

"I can't cancel it. Everyone is arriving today."

Iris took a deep breath. She completely understood where her friend was coming from. If she cancelled a televised wedding she was going to bring a lot of unwanted attention down on herself and Nick. "If you're not sure about Nick, then you should postpone things. You're going to spend the rest of your life with him."

She nodded. "I hate this. It's like when dad had that affair with that stupid eighteen-year-old. The media isn't going to be kind."

"Are you cancelling things?"

"I need to talk to Nick," she said.

"Okay. Do you want me to go with you?"

"No. I have to do this on my own," she said.

They both went their separate ways, Adler walking up to the house that Nick and she had purchased on the island and Iris walked back to the hotel. She started up the path toward the hotel, stopping at a bench to wipe her feet off and put her shoes back on. She took her phone out and glanced down to see that she'd missed a call from Quinn and one from Zac.

Good.

She wasn't ready to talk to Zac. She had to figure out how to pull herself back from what she'd admitted. From now on, she wasn't going to let her emotions get the better of her.

She texted Quinn and got back a call.

"Hey."

"Where are you?"

"On the beach, fixing to walk back to the hotel. Why?"

"Stay there," Quinn said. "I'm tracking you with the friend app, hold on."

She did as her friend asked, looking up at the sun. "Still there?"

"Yes, what's up? Did the media already start pinging you about Nick?"

"Yes. But that's not all. Something else has come up and it involves you."

"What?"

"Zac blurted out that you paid him to be with you this weekend in the lobby at the hotel. It was overheard by a bunch of reporters and everyone is running with the story."

"What?" Shock warred with anger and betrayal inside of her.

"Yeah, I know. Listen, it gets worse. Someone videoed him saying it on their phone, so everyone has it. There's no denying it," Quinn said.

"What am I going to do? I'm prelaunch on the new couples line. This affects everyone who works for me. My partnership deals," she said, but she stopped talking. Had Zac done it to prove he didn't love her? Had he thought that he needed to make it clear that things between them would end when the wedding weekend was over?

She was horrified and angry. She felt tears burning in her eyes as she fumbled in her bag for her sunglasses and put them on. She wasn't about to let him know how badly he'd hurt her. She texted her team to get another room at the hotel and meet her there in forty-five minutes. She was going to have to go on the offensive to save her business.

Quinn showed up a minute later and sat down next to her on the bench. She looked at her friend and all the betrayal and pain inside of her welled up. Quinn hugged her close.

"He's an idiot."

"He is," Iris agreed. "But I think I might have been the bigger one. I love him, Quinn."

"I know," her friend said. "I could tell last night."

"I'm going to have to spin this," she said.

"I think he cares for you too," Quinn started.

Iris shook her head. "It doesn't matter. We can't be together after this."

She hoped if she said the words out loud enough, her heart would get the message.

Zac didn't have the chance to talk to Iris before the rehearsal where she pretty much ignored him the entire time. Nick and Adler looked fragile and both went their separate ways after they were done. Zac wasn't sure what was going on between the two of them but he wanted to fix things with Iris.

He didn't blame her for ignoring him. Stephan

from her team had come to see him and had advised him that he wasn't needed for any promo or to do anything with Iris for the rest of the weekend.

He'd tried to talk to Stephan, but it was clear the other man wasn't having it. He'd left Zac feeling even worse about what had happened. And when he got to his grandmother's house, his entire family was tense. Even Mari, who usually found a way to lighten the mood, looked somber.

They were all gathered in the formal living room when Mari walked over to him and gave him a hug. "I love you, big bro, even though you are totally clueless sometimes."

"I'm not used to having anyone care what I say."

"But you knew she does," Mari said. "I like Iris a lot. I'm surprised at what you said, but I can see how it would be something she'd agree to. She's really smart about her brand and has been careful about how she manages it."

"Yeah, until I majorly messed it up. That wasn't my intent," Zac said. He'd spent all day thinking about the business side of it but he knew that if he'd handled the declaration of love better, they wouldn't be in this situation and she probably wouldn't care because she'd know he was on her side.

"No one thinks you did it intentionally," Mari said. "How are you going to make it up to her?"

He had a few ideas. So far none of them had been that great. He'd hoped he could talk to her. He knew that he was going to have to show her how much she meant to him. Make the big gesture and prove it to the world. His family was all for him doing something with Iris, anything that would take the spotlight off his father and the illegitimate son that no one had known about until yesterday.

Now that the media were beginning to hint they had the scoop on what had transpired at the Bissets' yesterday, Carlton was releasing a statement that had the backing of both the Williams and Bisset families. But no one believed that the scandal would go away that easily.

"I'm hoping that when the time is right…it will come to me."

Mari punched him in the shoulder. "Don't wing this, Zac. If she's important to you, then show her and make an effort."

"I am," he said. He had spent the entire day thinking of all of the things he'd learned about Iris since they'd met. It might not have been a long time but they'd both been real with each other. He was pretty sure he knew her better than anyone else.

He knew how badly he'd hurt her. He had humiliated her without meaning to and he knew he was going to have to bare his soul in order to have a chance at winning her back.

The rehearsal dinner was being held in the ballroom at his grandmother's house. It had been set with large round tables that would seat eight and a large dance floor in the middle. There was a live band and later on he knew that Toby Osborn was going to perform.

There was media at the event as Adler and Nick's

wedding was being filmed and most of the wedding guests were present. He had an idea and knew that if he was going to pull it off, he needed to get to work.

"Bye, kiddo. Wish me luck."

"Good luck," she said as he turned and walked out of the ballroom to find Toby. If there was a man who knew how to survive scandals, it was Adler's father. He didn't need advice because he knew what he needed to do, but he could use some backup.

He found Toby outside smoking a cigarette.

"Hey, I need your help. I'm not any good at this sort of thing and I screwed up royally with Iris."

"After last night? I thought you were going to propose," Toby said.

Drunk Zac had been prepared for that. Unfortunately that wasn't an option until he fixed things with Iris.

"Yes, I really messed up today. I want to do something that will show her what she means to me. Can you help me with some lyrics?" Zac asked. "I want to use the old song 'They Can't Take That Away From Me.' The song means something to us."

Toby listened to everything that Zac had to say and then nodded. "Okay. If that doesn't work, be prepared to grovel."

"I am," Zac said. And he was. He didn't want to lose Iris over this. Not when he'd finally realized that she was the person he wanted to always come home to. The one woman he needed to be his home port.

He told Toby what he wanted to say and the other man wrote it down, wordsmithing it as he went along. When they were done, he handed the paper to Zac who read over the words and hoped that Iris would understand that she was his world. She was the ocean underneath his yacht and he needed her.

He hurried into the ballroom. The band was almost ready to take a break but he asked them if they would stay and play for him while he sang for Iris.

They agreed and Zac took a deep breath.

"We have had an odd request and I hope you won't mind helping this man out by welcoming Zac Bisset to the stage. He has a special song he'd like to perform for Iris Collins."

Seventeen

The last thing Iris was interested in was seeing Zac dressed in a dinner jacket and tie looking way more handsome than someone who'd broken her heart should. She almost got up but Mari came over and put her hand on her shoulder.

"Give him a chance," she said. "If this doesn't make it right, then I'll be surprised."

She thought Mari was giving her brother too much credit but she sat back down and looked up at the stage.

"Thank you for allowing me to take the stage," Zac said. "Many of you may have heard about a pact that Iris and I made for the weekend and I'm sure you've inferred all sorts of things about it. But whatever you've come up with, it's not the truth. I'm sorry, Iris, for not being more careful when I spoke. I'm not used to the spotlight but that's no excuse. You asked me for a favor, which I agreed to and then broke my word. This in no way makes up for it, but I hope it will help you accept my apology. The sentiment is my own, the song is borrowed and the lyrics were tweaked by Toby Osborn."

He turned to the band and they started to play the beginning notes of "They Can't Take That Away From Me." She was flooded with memories of him dancing her around his living room and singing under his breath. That was the moment, she thought, when she'd first let her guard down and started to fall for him.

Zac started to sing in his off-key tone. He was singing the actual words of the song until he got to the chorus. Then she stopped breathing as he sang. Because the chorus was all about her and how he hoped she'd give him another chance.

He ended with, "Please don't take my angel face away."

Her heart was in her throat. Today had been long and she'd been through the wringer. But she'd missed him. Her manager had called and she'd done a live video on her YouTube channel talking honestly to her viewers, and it had resonated. A lot of them had made mistakes and understood how hard it was to find love. It had led to a good discussion, one Iris intended to keep going.

One of the brands she'd partnered with had

dropped her but Iris understood they needed someone who was perfect, not human like her.

He stood there on the edge of the risers waiting for her, and she hesitated for a second before she got up and walked over to him. The band started playing one more song as Zac led her to the corner of the ballroom.

"This morning when you said you loved me, it was buried in a bunch of other stuff and my foggy brain was still processing it when you walked out the door. I climbed down to the ground floor to go after you but…there you were, all you, and there I was, sloppy me in bare feet. And we both know you deserve better than that."

"No," she said. She could tell he still had more that he wanted to say but she wasn't going to let him go on believing she wanted more than him. "I think I made you feel like you wouldn't be good enough if you weren't fitting into my image of life, but I like life with you. I like me with you."

"I do too. I honestly am in love with you, but I feel like we could both use some time to believe it," he said. "I'm so sorry I blew our cover. I didn't mean to. For the first time in my life I was on rough seas and had no idea how to navigate myself through it. I realized after I blurted everything out to Logan that you are my keel, angel face. You keep me on course. I didn't know I needed that until we found each other."

"Me too. I love you, Zac. All of you. You embrace life in a way that I have never been comfortable allowing myself to. I guess I thought no one would accept me if I wasn't perfect but you have done that from the beginning."

Everyone applauded as he took her in his arms and kissed her.

A moment later there was a commotion and Iris looked up to see Adler pulling away from Nick and throwing her engagement ring at his feet.

"I can't do this," she said as she ran from the room.

* * * * *

*Will the Bisset scandal cost
Adler her happy ending?*

*You'll want to find out
when the One Night series
by* USA TODAY *bestselling author
Katherine Garbera continues soon...*

*Available exclusively
from Harlequin Desire.*

WE HOPE YOU ENJOYED
THIS BOOK FROM

⊞ HARLEQUIN
DESIRE

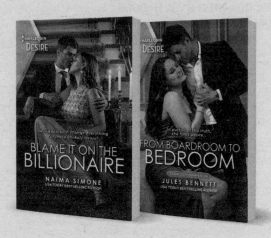

*Luxury, scandal, desire—welcome to
the lives of the American elite.*

Be transported to the worlds of oil barons, family dynasties,
moguls and celebrities. Get ready for juicy plot twists,
delicious sensuality and intriguing scandal.

6 NEW BOOKS AVAILABLE EVERY MONTH!

COMING NEXT MONTH FROM

DESIRE

Available May 5, 2020

#2731 CLAIMED BY A STEELE
Forged of Steele • by Brenda Jackson
When it comes to settling down, playboy CEO Gannon Steele has a ten-year plan. And it doesn't include journalist Delphine Ryland. So why is he inviting her on a cross-country trip? Especially since their red-hot attraction threatens to do away with all his good intentions...

#2732 HER TEXAS RENEGADE
Texas Cattleman's Club: Inheritance • by Joanne Rock
When wealthy widow and business owner Miranda Dupree needs a security expert, there's only one person for the job—her ex, bad boy hacker Kai Maddox. It's all business until passions reignite, but will her old flame burn her a second time?

#2733 RUTHLESS PRIDE
Dynasties: Seven Sins • by Naima Simone
Putting family first, CEO Joshua Lowell abandoned his dreams to save his father's empire. When journalist Sophie Armstrong uncovers a shocking secret, he'll do everything in his power to shield his family from another scandal. But wanting her is a complication he didn't foresee...

#2734 SCANDALOUS REUNION
Lockwood Lightning • by Jules Bennett
Financially blackmailed attorney Maty Taylor must persuade her ex, Sam Hawkins, to sell his beloved distillery to his enemy. His refusal does nothing to quiet the passion between Maty and Sam. When powerful secrets are revealed, can their second chance survive?

#2735 AFTER HOURS SEDUCTION
The Men of Stone River • by Janice Maynard
When billionaire CEO Quinten Stone is injured, he reluctantly accepts live-in help at his remote home from assistant Katie Duncan—who he had a passionate affair with years earlier. Soon he's fighting his desire for the off-limits beauty as secrets from their past resurface...

#2736 SECRETS OF A FAKE FIANCÉE
The Stewart Heirs • by Yahrah St. John
Rejected by the family she wants to know, Morgan Stewart accepts Jared Robinson's proposal to pose as his fiancée to appease his own family. But when their fake engagement uncovers real passion, can Morgan have what she's always wanted, or will a vicious rumor derail everything?

"Stalking me, Ms. Armstrong?" he drawled, his fingers gripping his water bottle so tight, the plastic squeaked in protest.

He immediately loosened his hold. Damn, he'd learned long ago to never betray any weakness of emotion. People were like sharks scenting bloody chum in the water when they sensed a chink in his armor. But when in this woman's presence, his emotions seemed to leak through like a sieve. The impenetrable shield barricading him that had been forged in the fires of pain, loss and humiliation came away dented and scratched after an encounter with Sophie. And that presented as much of a threat, a danger to him, as her insatiable need to prove that he was a deadbeat father and puppet to a master thief.

"Stalking you?" she scoffed, bending down to swipe her own bottle of water and a towel off the ground. "Need I remind you, it was you who showed up at my job yesterday, not the other way around. So I guess that makes us even in the showing-up-where-we're-not-wanted department."

"Oh, we're not even close to anything that resembles even, Sophie," he said, using her name for the first time aloud. And damn if it didn't taste good on his tongue. If he didn't sound as if he were stroking the two syllables like they were bare, damp flesh.

"I hate to disappoint you and your dreams of narcissistic grandeur, but I've been a member of this gym for years." She swiped her towel over her throat and upper chest. "I've seen you here, but it's not my fault if you've never noticed me."

"That's bull," he snapped. "I would've noticed you."

The words echoed between them, the meaning in them pulsing like a thick, heavy heartbeat in the sudden silence that cocooned them. Her silver eyes flared wide before they flashed with...what? Surprise? Irritation? Desire. A liquid slide of lust prowled through him like a hungry—so goddamn hungry—beast.

The air simmered around them. How could no one else see it shimmer in waves from the concrete floor like steam from a sidewalk after a summer storm?

She was the first to break the visual connection, and when she ducked her head to pat her arms down, the loss of her eyes reverberated in his chest like a physical snapping of tautly strung wire. He fisted his fingers at his side, refusing to rub the echo of soreness there.

"Do you want me to pull out my membership card to prove that I'm not some kind of stalker?" She tilted her head to the side. "I'm dedicated to my job, but I refuse to cross the line into creepy…or criminal."

He ground his teeth against the apology that shoved at his throat, but after a moment, he jerked his head down in an abrupt nod. "I'm sorry. I shouldn't have jumped to conclusions." And then because he couldn't resist, because it still gnawed at him when he shouldn't have cared what she—a reporter—thought of him or not, he added, "That predilection seems to be in the air."

She narrowed her eyes on him, and a tiny muscle ticked along her delicate but stubborn jaw. Why that sign of temper and forced control fascinated him, he opted not to dwell on. "And what is that supposed to mean?" she asked, the pleasant tone belied by the anger brewing in her eyes like gray storm clouds.

Moments earlier, he'd wondered if fury or desire had heated her gaze.

God help him, because masochistic fool that he'd suddenly become, he craved them both.

He wanted her rage, her passion…wanted both to beat at him, heat his skin, touch him. Make him feel.

Mentally, he scrambled away from that, that need, like it'd reared up and flashed its fangs at him. The other man he'd been—the man who'd lost himself in passion, paint and life captured on film—had drowned in emotion. Willingly. Joyfully. And when it'd been snatched away—when that passion, that life—had been stolen from him by cold, brutal reality, he'd nearly crumbled under the loss, the darkness. Hunger, wanting something so desperately, led only to the pain of eventually losing it.

He'd survived that loss once. Even though it'd been like sawing off his own limbs. He might be an emotional amputee, but dammit, he'd endured. He'd saved his family, their reputation and their business. But he'd managed it by never allowing himself to need again.

And Sophie Armstrong, with her pixie face and warrior spirit, wouldn't undo all that he'd fought and silently screamed to build.

Don't miss what happens next in…
Ruthless Pride *by Naima Simone,*
the first in the Dynasties: Seven Sins series,
where passion may be the only path to redemption.

Available May 2020 wherever
Harlequin Desire books and ebooks are sold.

Harlequin.com

HDEXP0420

4303